THE MAN WHO CAME FROM AWAY

a Cape Breton odyssey

JEREMY AKERMAN

author of

Black Around the Eyes

The Man who Came from Away: a Cape Breton Odyssey
© 2025 Jeremy Akerman

Cover design: Rebekah Wetmore
Cover image: a post card from the time of this story.
Editor: Andrew Wetmore

ISBN: 978-1-998149-91-9
First edition July 2025

Moose House Publications
2475 Perotte Road
Annapolis County, NS
B0S 1A0
moosehousepress.com
info@moosehousepress.com

Moose House Publications recognizes the support of the Province of Nova Scotia. We are pleased to work in partnership with the Department of Communities, Culture and Heritage to develop and promote our cultural resources for all Nova Scotians.

We live and work in Mi'kma'ki, the ancestral and unceded territory of the Mi'kmaw people. This territory is covered by the "Treaties of Peace and Friendship" which Mi'kmaw and Wolastoqiyik (Maliseet) people first signed with the British Crown in 1725. The treaties did not deal with surrender of lands and resources but in fact recognized Mi'kmaq and Wolastoqiyik (Maliseet) title and established the rules for what was to be an ongoing relationship between nations. We are all Treaty people.

Also by Jeremy Akerman

and available from Moose House Publications

Memoir
Outsider

Politics
What Have You Done for Me Lately? - revised edition

The Marc LeBlanc Mysteries
Holy Grail, Sacred Gold
Unspeakable Evil
The Plot to Kill the Premier
Best Served Cold
My Brother's Keeper

Fiction
Black Around the Eyes – revised edition
The Affair at Lime Hill
The Premier's Daughter
In Search of Dr. Dee
Explosion
Decline and Fall

This book is dedicated to the Town of Glace Bay,
which gave nearly 800 of its sons to fatal accidents
in the coal mines.
And to all its citizens, living and dead,
and especially to its many wonderful, colourful characters.

The story lines in this novel are fictional, although they are derived from actual experiences in a Cape Breton mining town.

The main characters, Winston Barber, The MacNeil family, Alex and Evangeline MacDonald, and the staff at the Melody Café, are fictional. All others were actual, living people who populated Glace Bay when the author was a young man.

Lonnie Kelly existed, but his name has been changed.

The Man who Came from Away

The Man who Came from Away

Jeremy Akerman

1

A few streaks of bright pink, delicately streaming from the eastern horizon, heralded the sun's first attempts to start the day. The Canso Causeway was deserted. Beyond, on the Cape Breton Island side, the land was still in dark shadow. Only a few pink-tipped tree-tops, and a forlornly flickering motel sign, were visible in the gloom.

It was the summer of 1970. Coal was still being mined on the island, but now only in three locations, by a workforce of fewer than 4,000 men. This was but a pathetic remnant of the industry in which, between the world wars, over 13,000 men were employed in twenty mines. Since mining began here in the eighteenth century, more than 300 mines had been sunk and worked. In that time, the extraction of over 300 millions tonnes of coal had claimed the lives of 2,584 men, and twenty times that number were injured.

Cape Breton was at the beginning of its slow decline as an economic and political force in Nova Scotia, although few knew it at the time. The steel plant in Sydney had been on a downward path for many years and now teetered on the brink of survival, the provincial government having recently taken ownership from the British firm, Hawker Siddeley.

This was not a time of general optimism. Cape Breton did not share the national enthusiasm for Canada's new, dashing Prime Minister, Pierre Trudeau, although they grudgingly re-elected long-time Liberal lion Alan MacEachen in a rural constituency, the other two ridings going to the Conservatives.

Unemployment was close to 10 percent and an increasing number of the Island's youth were moving to Ontario or to Alberta where McIntyre Coal Mines Ltd. was actively operating in the Smoky River mine field and Caw Ridge, and the town of Grand Cache was growing fast.

The coastal communities continued their traditional fishing occupations, and one of the largest make-work projects in Canadian history, the Fortress of Louisbourg, employed a few hundred people, although many of them were seasonal.

~

Winston Barber was a total stranger to Cape Breton and Nova Scotia, having been born and raised in small-town New Jersey and spent his working life in Los Angeles and New York. When he drove from Maine across the Canadian border two days ago, it was his first visit to what he had always imagined to be a cold, wintry vastness populated by Mounties and moose.

Winston was a tall, rangy, handsome man of 42, with a mouth whose upturned corners suggested a permanent smile. He had been many things in his short life, but for the past five years he had been in the film industry as a writer. Winston had private views about the screenplays on which he worked, and others he had seen, but did what was asked of him. He thought his industry was virtually bankrupt of ideas, incessantly repeating and reviving old themes, and that young men in suits were dominating—and killing —any creative energy capable of producing masterpieces of the screen like those which had been produced in bygone days.

Winston had been married only once, when he was twenty-two, to Irene, a sweet girl who had left him nine months after they had set up house. He did not really know—or care—why she went and had not been not especially sorry to see her go. Since then he had played the field and found he had a knack of attracting women and charming them with lines he would have liked to put in his scripts.

He had made few real friendships in Los Angeles, and even fewer in New York, because the personnel in his working environment often changed radically, and such spare time as his work allowed, he devoted to being nice to women and having them be nice to him. Thus, he was always kind, not inconsiderate and never brutal in these liaisons; and he felt it would be fair to say that the women benefited from the relationship as much, and in a similar way, as he did.

One firm friendship he had made was with Dan Petrie, a talented director with whom he had worked on several films. Dan had been born in Glace Bay, a town of some 20,000 on Cape Breton's northeast coast, in the centre of its coalfield. Dan told him he wanted to make a movie about this home town and had asked him to spend some time there and come back with ideas for a screenplay.

Since he had just finished a project and had not yet acquired another one, Winston had agreed to Dan's request. After dickering about the remuneration and length of the endeavour, they had shaken hands and parted. The next day, Winston had packed his bags, hopped into his Corvette and headed north.

The mainland side of the causeway was in even deeper shade than the Cape Breton boundary, and the looming blackness of the quarry hill opposite was barely silhouetted against the inky blue sky. What was once Porcupine Mountain had, for over twenty years, been gradually eroded by giant machines in order, first, to provide tons of material to build the causeway, and thereafter to furnish a vast amount of gravel for the province's roads. Now the mountain's top had gone and a huge gash had appeared in its side.

The stuttering light of the motel sign picked out a number of parked cars, one of them Winston's Corvette sporting New York plates. Apart from the faulty, flashing sign, in the motel a single light shone weakly through the plastic, flowered curtains of one of the units.

While the seven other temporary occupants of the motel were still slumbering, inside Winston's unit the sheets were thrown back, and the surface of the bed was strewn with a half packed suitcase, piles of neatly folded clothes, and a typewriter in its battered case.

In the tiny bathroom—with no bath—Winston tried to shave with the aid of a mirror covered in small, mysterious, brown spots. Between the mirror's discolorations, Winston examined his tanned, still-youthful, face with its sparkling blue eyes and per-petual, incipient grin. He was lucky, he knew, to have been blessed with a fine face and a fit, lithe body. He had kept in shape, but to a large extent it was a matter of luck, because his slightly elder brother, Syme, was, it had to be admitted, quite ugly and, despite his running and weight training, was a poor specimen of manhood.

As he shaved, slowly and methodically, Winston thought about his journey from New York to Nova Scotia. He had observed mil-lions of spruce trees, a great many fields, mostly grass, but some with crops, and glimpses of the gleaming sea revealed piecemeal as the road bent and twisted.

As he approached Cape Breton, he had seen low mountain ranges like immense, slumbering, prehistoric beasts; evanescent fields; blue-hazed woodlands and placid, meandering rivers. It seemed a lulling, luring place, and long before he crossed the Canso Causeway he felt he had entered a land time had forgotten.

Frantic, slithering, silver streams flowed on either side of the road, and thick, storybook, cauliflower trees rolled steeply up to a roofless sky. Threading between romantically precipitous slopes, he had almost gone off the road whilst craning to see the crests of the valley, and a truck coming from behind gave him a long, wailing, accusative blast.

During a restless night caused by dreams of walking woods and singing waterfalls, and a flickering neon light relentlessly penetrating the plastic curtain, he was pestered by a single mosquito. Winston was impelled to get out of bed and, holding a rolled newspaper, tried to hunt the insect down. Several times he thought he had dispatched it and returned to bed, only to hear the soft whining of its wings circling around his head yet again.

He pulled the sheet over his head, but found that this not only prevented him from breathing properly, but also gave no protection from the creature. Two swelling bites told him that the mosquito had accomplished her devilish penetration through the cotton.

The sound of his small travel clock alarm had caused Winston to rise very early, and he hoped to get on the road before sunrise.

2

The sky was lightening as the bright pink from the horizon spread, suffusing the landscape with a magical, rosy wash. Looking admiringly about him, Winston left his unit in the motel and walked to his car. He loaded his belongings into the trunk, slammed the door shut, and climbed in behind the wheel, snuggling himself into the saddle leather seat.

He placed his hands on the leather-covered steering wheel and imagined what it would be like to pilot an F-15, or a Mirage III, the French single-engine, supersonic fighter aircraft known for its manoeuvrability and advanced technology.

Once he had applied to join the U.S. Air Force, but was rejected on account of a small bone spur on the underside of his acromion, which the doctor said could, at extreme speeds, cause shoulder difficulty with activities which involved overhead movement of the arms. So his chance to fly an F-15, let alone a Mirage III, vanished and would not come again.

He started the car, switched on the interior light and spread a map on the passenger seat. With his index finger he traced his proposed route up Highway 4, along the eastern shore of the Bras D'Or lakes, through the island's largest town, Sydney, and to his final destination, Glace Bay.

He gently pulled the Corvette out of the parking lot and headed eastwards into what was now a blood-red sunrise. He attempted to remember the old verse, but could not recall whether the red sky he was witnessing was a good or bad omen.

By the time it was fully light, the morning was as close to being perfect as was possible. The lakes were almost blinding as pin-point reflections on the tips of the waves twinkled and glistened brightly. The greens of trees, fields and rolling hills unfolded before him. In some of the fields, a few horses peered curiously as he passed. In others, cows briefly glanced up from the dewy grass. The sheep he occasionally encountered paid him no attention.

Every now and then a revealed inlet from the lakes gave views of comfortable old houses with stacks of cordwood against their outer walls, small jetties, and boats in blues, reds and greens at anchor nearby. On the hilly south side of the road, grey, weathered farm houses appeared, some with their barns barely clinging to an upright life, and their yards littered with rusty, outdated and outworn implements.

In a softly-glowing, somewhat-intoxicating reverie, Winston wound his away along the gleaming lakes, through tiny, trim villages and scattered native reserves, past old creaking cabins and occasional gashes in the forest where cutting had taken place, until eventually he reached the rural suburbs of Sydney, and the mining towns beyond.

3

About the time Winston was passing through Cleveland on Highway 4 in Richmond County, some 140 kilometres away the sun was rising on a different road. This thoroughfare was Upper Dominion Street, or Number Three Hill, as it was usually called by the local inhabitants, one of the four roads leading into the settlement heralded on a large sign on the grass verge:

WELCOME TO GLACE BAY.

The road got its name from an ancient slope mine located on the outcrop of the Phalen Seam in the Passchendaele area of the town, which was opened in 1900. The seam in this area was 7 feet, 6 inches thick and worked on a pillar and room system, and was in continuous operation until 1915, when it was closed. During its life the colliery produced almost four million tons of coal from an area extending over 492 acres.

The redness had gone from the sun now, and only a suggestion of pink still lingered in the sky. Fingers of brass-yellow light peered over the edge of the sea and stabbed forward over the sleeping town and up this hill. Next to the sign, a beam of light captured a large, dirty, white cat frozen in position as it blinked into the new sun. It sniffed the air for a few seconds, then padded across the road.

As the cat drew near to the edge of the pavement, the sound of loud snoring assailed its ears. The creature crept forward and peered through the long grass, soiled by exhaust fumes and the ubiquitous coal dust which permeated the environs.

In the bottom of the ditch it observed the dishevelled figure of one of the town's most obstreperous, colourful drunks. Raggedly dressed, unkempt and unwashed, this was Lonnie Kelly, a rangy, weather-beaten man of indeterminate age. He was unshaven and had long, filthy hair, terrifying, bloodshot eyes and broken, yellow teeth.

His clothing might once have been smart and bright, but that was many years since, and now it was button-less, torn, and stained by a thousand spilled drinks and remnants of meals, and almost as many pungent incidents of vomitus. The chill of the air had caused Lonnie to pull the tattered jacket around him, but it had fallen open to reveal that, underneath, he wore no shirt.

The ditch was quite wide, so, in order to attain the further bank, the cat planned to use Lonnie's body as a springboard. It jumped, landed on an excessively hairy belly matted with dirt, and there it paused before attempting its second leap.

The pressure of its feet caused Lonnie to awaken with a start and violently sweep away the cat with his arm.

"Frig off you jeesly bastard!" he roared.

The cat propelled itself to the other bank and rapidly disappeared into the undergrowth, only to emerge on the road a little distance away.

Moaning hoarsely, Lonnie slowly roused himself, shakily stood up and perfunctorily brushed the loose grass and soil from his clothes. He squinted into the slowly-strengthening sun and, looking out from his temporary abode, perceived the town below. The light was now catching the roofs of the taller buildings, picking out schools, churches and pitheads.

While the cat watched him warily from a safe distance, Lonnie scrambled up the bank and, with unconcerned abandon, proceeded to copiously relieve himself. This function fulfilled, he searched his few pockets and withdrew a cigarette butt and a match. With great difficulty and shaking hands he managed to light the stub and gave it a few furious puffs before casting it away.

Then, lumbering unsteadily, Lonnie made his way down the hill towards the community of Passchendaele, known to its inhabitants as Number 11. This, too, had been a colliery of the Dominion Coal Company, begun in 1899 and closed in 1949, producing over seven million tonnes in its lifetime.

As Lonnie plodded downwards, far in the distance the sun was now illuminating a flat promontory protruding into the sea. On this headland sat about a hundred aging company houses originally built around an undersea mine, Number 7, which had operated from 1861 until 1874. This community was named after the seam of coal that colliery mined: The Hub.

4

The Hub was an area of Glace Bay comprising six parallel streets running north-south. When it was laid out by the coal company in the nineteenth century, like those of its neighbours in New Aberdeen, the streets were given numbers, not names. These were intersected at right angles by four other streets.

At the time of Winston's visit, almost all habitations here were company houses built primarily between 1850 and 1920, initially by The General Mining Association, which held a monopoly on Nova Scotia minerals from 1827 to 1857 under the titular ownership of the Duke of York.

Considering the coal company's parsimony in other respects, these dwellings, built to house miners and their families, were constructed of remarkably stout materials, some of the buildings surviving to the period of Winston's arrival.

Most of the company houses in Glace Bay were built during the period of greatest rapid industrial growth at the turn of the century, and in most cases were sold to the miners who lived in them, commencing after World War II. They were small duplexes or single-family homes, often ranging between 700 and 1,000 square feet, with two bedrooms upstairs and a kitchen and large room downstairs.

The colliery at the Hub Shaft opened in 1861 and was the first of the larger mines in Glace Bay. The first Hub Shaft had to be closed in 1872 due to fire, a perennial problem, but the seam itself continued to be mined for years to come.

That seam is believed to have yielded the first coal to be mined in the province, although that distinction is disputed by Port Morien, some miles down the coast. This coal was intended to supply the Fortress of Louisbourg, some forty-two miles away by sea, the only means of transporting it in the 1720s.

The British worked the mine during their tenure of Louisbourg and, in 1748, built a blockhouse named Fort William to protect the mine from Mi'kmaq attacks.

The French assumed control of the fort after the Treaty of Aix-la-Chapelle in 1748, which returned Louisbourg to its original owners, and under their control the colliery remained active until 1752, when a fire, which continued to burn until 1764, destroyed both the mine and the fort.

In the 1860s, mining on land was succeeded by perilous undersea operations, but another fire forced those efforts to close in 1872. Three years later the mine was flooded in order to finally extinguish the inferno.

The newly formed Dominion Coal Company reopened the mine in 1895, but closed it again in 1899 due to fears about safety and the thinness of the seam. In 1903, they opened a new mine, which they dubbed Dominion No. 7, only to have another fire cause operations to cease again. This misfortune gave rise to considerable resentment and charged emotions when the causes of the fire were hotly disputed, management blaming workers and *vice versa*.

The fire being out of control, the company decided it had no option but to, again, flood the mine to extinguish the flames. This was a controversial decision, and there followed a long, dramatic struggle to overcome the blaze, in which severe damage was done to equipment and buildings.

Mining recommenced in 1907, but ten years later it was closed for good. Company records indicate that the mine had yielded over two million tons of coal from slopes extending some 9,000 feet beneath the ocean.

There were no trees or tall buildings on this flat peninsula, so any sea winds coming off the ocean here seemed to be stronger and colder than they would be downtown. Some chip boxes and candy wrappers blew around fence posts, and the ashes of an overturned bucket were indiscriminately sprayed across the road surface. At this hour of the day, only a few mangy dogs sniffing around a garbage can were the only signs of life on the streets, but wisps of smoke starting from some chimneys indicated that some denizens of the Hub were stirring.

From a house at the end of one of the rows, the figure of a man emerged, climbed into a pickup truck, started the engine, and moved into the street, round the corner, and down another street, and pulled up outside an identical dwelling to the one he had left. This was the MacNeil residence, which accommodated some of the characters who were to play important roles in Winston Barber's sojourn in Glace Bay.

Mikey, the driver of the truck, gave a single, sharp blast on his horn, whereupon Donnie MacNeil, a short, well-built miner in his mid-thirties, appeared at the front door, and walked to the truck. He wore a baseball cap, heavy boots and old jeans. He carried a lunch can and yesterday's *Cape Breton Post*. Over a thick plaid work shirt he wore a jacket bearing the letters DEVCO, the acronym designating the Cape Breton Development Corporation, the federal crown corporation currently operating the area's mines.

Donnie on board, the truck pulled away, heading for Number 26 colliery three kilometres to the west. Going along Connaught Avenue, they passed a van, CAPE BRETON POST on its side, making for central Glace Bay, where the boy in the back would hurl bundles of newspapers though the swinging door onto the sidewalks outside various retail outlets.

In the other half of the MacNeils' duplex, Alex MacDonald heard Mikey's truck pull off. He pushed aside the yellowed lace curtains in the front room to watch it go. He was a tall, trim man in his early fifties, with a tanned, lined, face and bright blue eyes. Formerly a merchant mariner and coal miner, he wore a blue denim shirt and jeans.

Alex glanced across the dusty street in search of a face in the house opposite.

Sure enough, a little girl, Margie, was peering out of an upstairs window, and she gave Alex a cheery wave. She was nine and had thin, mousy hair, a sad, sickly, pale face and large, watery brown eyes. Alex waved back, then let the curtains fall and walked out of the room to the foot of the stairs.

"You awake yet, Ma?" he called up. "Do you want your tea now?"

"Yeah, alright, if it's made. Come up, b'y," replied his mother.

Her room's only ornamentation was to be found in a few cheap ceramic animals on the mantle and two holy pictures hanging on plain white walls; one of Jesus with a bright red sacred heart, and another of Mary, also with a visible heart, but this time of gold. Evangeline MacDonald lay in what seemed far too small a bed, and when she rolled over almost fell out. She grasped her ample bosom and coughed.

Evangeline was a very large woman of 90 summers, with a fleshy face and wispy, yellowish-white hair. She had been born a Fougère in the French settlement of Cheticamp, far away on the other side of the island, and had grown up there. When she was sixteen she had met Albert, Alex's father, at a fair in Port Hawkesbury at the Strait of Canso, and had been captivated by his racy talk of strikes and the coming revolution. Albert was long dead and now, 74 years later, yet waiting for that revolution, she still spoke with a strong Acadian accent.

From next door, through the thin walls, came the sound of Donnie's father, Murdoch MacNeil, snoring like an express train coming through the station on the down line. The china animals, one a dog, and one which looked like a cross between a cow and a rhinoceros, shook with a little tinkle with each of Murdoch's exhalations.

Alex gingerly carried a cup of tea and placed it on a small bedside table. "There you are, Ma. Here's your tea."

"Tanks, b'y. My, dat Murdoch is kickin' up some racket next door. I couldn't sleep no more wid that goin' on."

Unlike its counterpart on the other side of the duplex, the room in which Murdoch was thundering was full of clutter, and the walls and the top of a small dresser were crowded with artificial flowers, fading photographs of children and bronzed baby shoes. In the big double bed, so large there is space in the room for little other furniture, Murdoch and his wife, Katie, were sleeping.

Murdoch was a barrel-chested man in his eighties, with a craggy face and a mop of thick, snowy-white hair. Katie, his younger by some ten years, was a small—almost tiny—round woman with short, grey hair and a shiny, unlined, red-apple-skin face. They had been married for over half a century, their union having been blessed with Rita, the eldest; Dorothy in Toronto; Donnie; and much-loved Rosaline, who had died many years ago and about whom nobody was allowed to speak.

Rita pushed the bedroom door open quietly and timidly poked her head around the door. At first glance, she was a seemingly-mousy woman about forty, with long, straight, chestnut hair perpetually obscuring most of her pale face. She was considered locally to be the proverbial shy Old Maid, and seemed to do little to counteract this notion, walking with hunched shoulders and her head down. She wore a loose-fitting, nondescript grey gown and holey slippers which were too big for her.

Seeing her parents were still asleep, she gently withdrew, silently closed the door, crept along the landing and tip-toed downstairs to the kitchen. Here she lit the stove, filled a kettle and put it on the flame to boil. Feeling a little orange cat rub against her legs, Rita bent down and gave the creature a few strokes.

"You hungry, pussycat? I'll get you something."

She took a can of cat food from the cupboard, spooned its contents into a bowl over the big sink, and placed it on the floor.

The cat busily burrowed into the food, while Rita looked out of the window. From what she could see, she was convinced it was going to be a fine day.

5

The sun's progress was palpable and had spread to all but the forest's floor and the earth's most shadowy places. From the somnolent, evergreen hills of Inverness and Victoria counties to the quiet waters of the snake-like Mira River, to the orange-smoke-belching Sydney Steel plant, it was clear that day had broken and was here to stay, at least for another fourteen hours.

The *Cape Breton Post* van continued its relentless zig zag across the town, bumping through potholes and over street debris, and slowing only slightly past each store. In the back of the van, the boy performed his duties, seemingly bent on making as much noise and creating as much damage as possible, and at each place he hurled the bundles of newspapers with increasing force and savagery.

Flocks of seagulls wheeled in from the water, screeching and fighting for pizza crusts, and—who knew why—fiercely contended for torn pieces of cardboard strewn in the gutters. A few lucky crows which had found an unlidded garbage bin in which to forage, soon became unlucky as the gulls espied their discovery and attacked *en masse*, scattering the crows to the croaking winds.

Here and there, empty bottles, a few glasses and a legion of cigarette butts testified to gatherings on the streets prior to and after spending hours drinking in the Manor, Iggy's, and the Pithead taverns. These were not merely drunken assemblies for the purpose of insulting and occasionally fighting each other, but were parliaments of high debate. They considered such weighty subjects as which coalface was being opened next in Number 26, what had really happened to Ally Neary's missing wife, if several officers of the town's police had stolen television sets from a warehouse near the quay, and whether Bob Stanfield would have done better to stay in Nova Scotia than go to Ottawa and be outclassed by that slippery Frenchman, Trudeau.

As Lonnie Kelly turned onto Brookside Street into Caledonia, a district also named after its most famous mine, it was still quiet, with only a few vehicles passing. When a curious, adventurous, khaki-coloured dog ran out from behind a hedge and started nipping at Lonnie's ankles, he cursed and kicked it away. The dog backed into a gateway and snarled at his assailant, angrily watching him leave the scene.

Further on down the street, Lonnie paused and, leaning on a fence, loudly hawked, the spittle swaying from his chin. He rubbed his dirty hand over his bristly face, then tottered forward towards the town. The *Cape Breton Post* van came speeding out of Park Street, the driver loudly blowing its horn, and, as Lonnie staggered out of its path, the boy in the back jeered at him and made an indecent gesture.

Some 75 kilometres away, in Irish Cove, a sparsely-populated community on the shores of the shimmering Bras D'Or lakes, Winston Barber pulled his car off the road and climbed out to witness an impressive sight. He breathed deeply the fresh breeze, and narrowed his eyes against the almost blinding brightness of the sun on the vast expanse of barely-moving water. Far out, he thought he could just discern a small fishing boat, but immediately it disappeared into the glittering horizon. To his right, a few kilometres across the bay, Winston could just see through the haze a landmass which he would later learn was Castle Bay and, just beyond it, the Eskasoni Mi'kmaq Reserve.

After some minutes of watching three unidentified birds competing in a display of aerobatics, and feeling the delicious warmth of the rays on his skin, Winston reluctantly returned to his car and continued his journey eastwards up the side of a ten-mile inlet called East Bay.

As he gently cruised along, Winston thought it was good to be alive.

6

One street over from the MacNeil residence was an identical house, but in a better state of repair and recently painted. Other houses in the area had paint work which either cleaved to the original dark browns and greens given them by the coal company, or used bright reds, blues and occasionally a mustard yellow. But this house stood out because it was painted a feminine pale pink, with baby blue trim, and had expensive, flowery curtains at its ground floor windows. It was the residential equivalent of attempting to make a silk purse out of a sow's ear, but was the pride and joy of Annie Pyke.

While the house was not hers, but her father, Arthur's, she ruled the roost with a firm but condescending hand, tut-tutting as she fluttered, rearranged, plumped and, incessantly moved Arthur's favourite things to irritatingly unfavourite places. She saw to it that the grass in front of the house was always mown and manicured and that the pastel-coloured flowers were neatly weeded. Some other houses had picket fences, but none so upright, so clean, so white as hers.

The front door was one of a kind, and seemed particularly out of character in a place like the Hub because it had noble, if not royal, pretensions far above what might seem appropriate in a working class neighbourhood. To the door had been applied fake mouldings and artificial panels, and it was painted in an incongruous gold. By the street, Annie had her father, against his better judgment, erect a delicate white post topped by a black metal mailbox with gold scrolling, again suggesting the occupants within had claims to aristocratic connections.

Two of the upstairs windows boasted delicate white, frilly curtains, these being Annnie's bedroom; and a further window, hung with a plain, brown drape, indicated the location of Arthur's nocturnal quarters. The rule had never actually been laid down by fiat, but in that mysterious, intangible way she had, Annie had rendered it clear that the occupant of neither room should, under any circumstances, enter that of the other.

Thus it was that as Annie sat at her mirror that morning, she was certain that no earthly eye, other than her own, had ever beheld this bastion of pink, puffed and powdered femininity. The room was over-decorated with flowered wallpaper, pastel-coloured furniture, a flouncy bed with more frills, teddy bears, dolls and a host of other knick-knacks and mementos.

Wearing a pink dressing gown with a synthetic fur collar, she applied her make-up to the accompaniment of her own humming and the strains of CJCB Radio.

Annie Pyke was a trim, pink, fine-figured blonde in her early thirties. While she could not be described as beautiful, she was attractive in a slightly hard way, her aggressiveness at home and her ambition at work having given edges to her softness. Her clothes came not from Toby's, Lipkus' Rukashin's, Marshall's or Rosenblum's on Commercial Street in Glace Bay, but from the Smart Shop in Sydney, where Harvey Webber always flattered her and treated her like a lady, but where she paid more than was necessary. She was always smartly attired, even in her work clothes, and wherever she went she made sure people could see the large engagement ring on her finger. This, purchased at Alteen's jewellers on Charlotte Street in Sydney, had cost her fiancé, Donnie MacNeil, over two months' wages, and because he was not able to pay for it outright, Annie had given him the money and he had repaid her in monthly instalments.

Downstairs, in a shiny, spotless kitchen equipped with the most modern appliances, Annie's father sat at a side table next to a wide open window. Listening intently for imminent footsteps on the stairs, Arthur furtively smoked a hand-made roll-up, leaned over and blew the fumes out into the garden. He wiped a small dew drop from his large, aquiline nose, and sniffed.

He watched a tiny dog, of indeterminate pedigree, run round and round a mysterious object at the edge of the street. Finally the dog grew bored and ran off. Arthur stared hard, but still could not identify what it was that had commanded the animal's attention.

Arthur Pyke was a tall, thin, rangy man in his late seventies with a long, lugubrious, horse-like face whose nose did not seem to belong with the rest of his physiognomy. His thinning hair was still brownish in places, being white only around his ears, and his jutting lower lip invariably prevented him from completely shaving the bristles lurking below. When he sucked in the smoke from his roll-up, his cheeks hollowed so that they almost touched in the middle of his mouth. When he exhaled, he continued to blow long after the smoke had departed, creating a small whistle.

Hearing the sound of Annie's bedroom door closing, Arthur stuck his arm out of the window, stubbed his cigarette on the outside wall and allowed the stub to drop to the earth beneath. Making a mental note to push the soil over to hide the butt later, he furiously waved the curtain back and forth to disperse any residual smell.

The kitchen door opened and Annie, now dressed for work, entered, paused at the opening, wrinkled her nose and shot a disappointed, censorious glance at her father.

"Good morning, Dad. Are we alright?"

Whenever Annie spoke to her father she did so in a patronizing tone suggestive of a nanny addressing a small child, rather than a man twice her age. Often she referred to him in the plural, as if this would cajole him into doing as he she wished. Her asking, "How are we feeling today?" or, "Are we going for a walk today?" particularly annoyed him, but he never complained; he knew it would achieve nothing.

"Oh, there you are, dear. Everything okay?"

"Heavens, there's an awful stink in here." Annie did a pirouette. "Did something die in here, or what?"

"Maybe it's that fish you cooked last night," Arthur suggested weakly.

"The fish? Right!"

Annie bustled about, plugging in the kettle, getting milk from the fridge, and setting out cups. While this domestic ritual was being performed, Arthur sat silently, staring at his hands. Noticing a nicotine stain on a finger he made a fist and put his other hand on top of it.

"Where are we off to today?"

"Oh, round and about. I guess I'll drop by the Pensioners' Union a bit later."

"That old Pensioners' Union! Beating your gums for hours along with that Murdoch MacNeil, I shouldn't wonder. All the scallywags in town get together down there. I suppose you think you're solving the problems of the world."

"Something like that, dear. I don't say much meself, but I likes to listen to the others shootin' off. Murdoch is right good, and Danny the Dancer always puts on a good show."

"Danny the Dancer!" Annie was indignant. "Now, there's a fellow with the tall tales, right enough. What other reprobates goes down there?"

"Angus Blue."

"Blue? Oh, my God. He'll give you a good laugh."

"That's for sure. I heard the priest asked him why he hadn't been to church lately, and Blue told him it was because he'd become a Communionist! Father Allen asked him what in the name of time a Communionist was and Angus said he didn't rightly know, but he knew they didn't go to church."

"Hah! Isn't he the one who hollered at the kids at the Little League dinner, 'Shut up, you little Christers and eat your frigging banquet!'?"

"That's him."

"I can see you're going to have a more entertaining day than me."

"Possibly so."

"Alright, I'm off to work. And, Dad…"

"What?"

"Don't be doing anything foolish, will you?"

"As if I would," Arthur said regretfully.

7

The sun was well up now, and had chased almost every wisp of cloud out of the sky. A rustling breeze from the sea crept around every corner, disarranging dust and convulsing candy wrappers and cigarette packages on the sidewalks.

From a doorway alongside Markadonis' shoe emporium, propelled by an unknown hand, a bag of garbage hurtled into the gutter. Instantly a screeching gull swooped at the bag and started tearing it to pieces as other gulls clattered in to share the pickings. They wheeled and squawked and cackled as they thrashed about on the sidewalk, the contents of the bag and their feathers flying indiscriminately.

A few people, Annie Pyke among them, walked to their places of work. With the exception of store clerks, bank managers, professionals, and gas station attendants, these were women, the older ones moving with a kind of shuffle, the younger ones with the click-clack of high heels.

As this was an area experiencing 12% unemployment, many men had not left their houses and sat on their front steps, smoking, gazing into the distance. The majority of the men who did have jobs had long since reported to their employers, and the miners were already half a mile out under the sea. Some shopkeepers were taking down the protective grilles from their front windows. At other windows, they were busy cleaning and polishing.

Bruce Sterns was opening The Medical Hall when Phil Simon

passed by on his way to a day of gassing and extracting, drilling and filling, and all with ancient equipment and great empathy. Nobody in Glace Bay liked going to the dentist, but everybody in Glace Bay liked Phillip Simon.

Phil thought that if, as usual, Bruce made a joke about pulling teeth, he would respond with a comment about a Kansas City pharmacist who got thirty years in jail for diluting 100,000 prescriptions and was responsible for the deaths of over 4,000 patients.

In the event, Bruce was too engaged in attempting to remove a large stain on his door to exchange more than a quick greeting, so Phil tucked the story away in the back of his memory for use on another occasion.

Max Lubetsky, stood in the doorway of his furniture store and cheerily waved to a woman passing on the other side of the street.

"Good morning, Mrs. Morrison," he called, "It's a wonderful day."

"You're right there Mr. Lubetsky," replied the woman with a twinkle. "I don't guess too many'll be buying tables and chesterfields today."

"Hmm." Max looked up at the clear azure ceiling, stretching further than he could see. He sighed. "I might as well close up and go fishing."

"Haha. Somehow I don't think you'll be doing that, Mr. Lubetsky."

"Indeed he will not," said his wife, Anita, appearing behind him. "Nobody never paid any bills going fishing!"

Max grinned sheepishly.

"Now get in here, Max, and move this roll of lino."

The *Cape Breton Post* van zoomed past. The boy in the back propelled a bundle of newspapers at the doorway of the Melody Café. Annie noted with approval that the projectile did not appear to be damaged, as she intended to sell all copies of *The Post* that day.

As she approached the door of the café, Lonny Kelly lurched

round Senators' Corner from Union Street and made an ill judged landing on Commercial Street at Annie's feet. She backed away with obvious distaste.

"Hello, darlin'," he slurred. "You openin' up now? Give me a cuppa tea, will ya?."

"Get!" Annie barked. "Get goin', Lonnie, before I calls the cops."

Kelly stumbled across the street, narrowly avoiding a passing coal truck. He stood swaying for several minutes, trying to decide in which direction he should go next. He spat in the gutter, clumsily hitched up his filthy pants, and headed up towards Main Street.

Annie unlocked the Melody Café, methodically picked up the bundle of newspapers, cut the string, put the papers in a rack, took off her light summer coat, hung it up in the back room, put on her apron, plugged in the coffee urns, filled the filters with coffee, took bread, butter, bacon and eggs from the fridge, pulled up the window blinds, turned on the lights, took a quick turn around the floor with a broom, reversed the Closed sign on the door, and assumed her position of preeminence behind the counter, preparatory to the arrival of her devoted and obedient staff.

8

The sun was hot when Winston Barber's car negotiated the out-skirts of the City of Sydney. He stopped at a gas station and had his tank refilled as he leaned against the scorching metal of the vehicle. The attendant was loquacious and friendly, but Winston had some difficulty in fully understanding him because he was un-familiar with the Cape Breton dialect.

"I need directions. Can you help me please?"

"Sure, whatchu wanna know?"

"First, I need to go to something called Xavier College."

"Well, now I come to think on it, there's two of them colleges. For one of them, you goes straight through town here and when you gets to the udder side, there she is on the right."

"Thanks."

"Wait now, b'y. There's anudder one on George Street in town."

"I want the history department."

"Jeez, I don't know about that. Could be either one, I guess."

The attendant told Winston his name was Kenny and that he lived in a place called Whitney Pier. As far as Winston was able to follow his speech, he came from one of thousands of families named MacDonald on Cape Breton, and was the third of seven brothers.

"That's a large family," said Winston.

"Yeah, seven, and one dead."

"Dead?"

"Yeah." Kenny said it with a sharp aspiration of his breath, something Winston later discovered was a common trait on the Island. "Yeah. A little one died at the beginning."

"I'm so sorry."

"Thass alright, b'y. Happened 'fore I come along."

Kenny told Winston his father had been working in the nail mill at the steel plant, but had been injured so was "on the comp." This, Kenny explained, was Workmen's Compensation, which was a provincial scheme devised to protect employers from civil lawsuits. In return for surrendering the right to sue, the injured parties could claim benefits according to an elaborate scheme of payments. Kenny's father, Gus, had lost two fingers in a work accident, so in addition to receiving an amount for a limited period, he would get a small lump sum.

"The Compensation Board uses what we calls the 'meat chart' with the dollar amount alongside each part of the body. So there's so much you gets from losing a finger. So much for toes, so much for an arm, and so on."

"What about lung diseases?" Winston asked. "I imagine they must be common at the plant with that dirty, orange smoke I see."

"Thass dust, not smoke, b'y. In the mornin's you sees it on all the cars parked in the street. One day it was coverin' the flowers at my Nan's place. Me Ma told me to go over and wipe it off."

"Did you go?"

"Like fuck, I did." Kenny laughed. "But there's worse diseases the miners gets. Sillycolosis. Something like that."

"How does the Compensation Board treat men with silicosis?"

"Not so good. The men has to be able to show that any disability they got was caused by workin' the pit."

"Why is that a problem?"

"Cuz if any of the men smokes—and they pretty near all do—the board says thass what caused their lung problems."

"Ah, I see how that could present difficulties."

"You got that right."

"Tell me, how big was the steel plant originally?"

"When I was a little feller—I was born in 1948—there was something like 6,000 men workin' there. I heard tell that over a third of all iron and steel makin' in Canada was done in Sydney."

Kenny said that even when his father was fit to return to work, his job might have disappeared because the nail mill was already being phased out. He told Winston that the steel plant had heavily relied on the production of steel rails for CN and other railroads, making it vulnerable to changes in the world's transportation systems. When the market shifted, the plant's reliance on outdated equipment and its lack of diversification into other steel products also furthered its rapid decline. That was why, Kenny said, the private owners had been only too willing to unload the plant on to the Nova Scotia government.

"Thank you, Kenny. You're a real encyclopedia. Could you recommend a restaurant where I could get some breakfast?"

"Thass no problem, b'y. Jasper's is just up here on the right. You can't miss it." He added, "Me Ma works there. She's the fat one with the big mouth." He laughed uproariously

The man's directions were accurate, and soon Winston saw the Jasper's sign. He parked in the lot and went in. He was surprised to see it was almost full and that there were about forty people tucking into enormous plates of food.

Winston took a copy of the *Cape Breton Post* from the end of the counter and sat down at the only empty table.

At the far end of the restaurant he could see a waitress who fitted Kenny's description of his mother, since she was large and her voice echoed throughout the room. He turned to his newspaper, skimmed the front page, then amused himself by reading letters to Ann Landers.

"Do yez know what yez want?"

Winston looked up to see an attractive teenager wearing a white blouse, brown skirt and frilly apron.

"Oh, no. What do you recommend?"

"I dunno." The girl giggled. "How 'bout the Big Breffast? Thass right poplar."

"What's that like?"

"Big." The girl giggled again.

"I mean what's included?"

"Three eggs, bacon, sausages, home fries, toast, coffee…"

"That sounds good. I can't guarantee I'll finish it all, but I'll give it a try."

And very good it was, too. Winston ate almost the whole plateful, took his time, and perused the newspaper from end to end. He read that G. I. Smith, who had taken over as premier from Robert Stanfield two years earlier, was reported to be considering holding a provincial election. The last election had been in 1967, when Stanfield had won 40 seats in the legislature to the young Liberal leader, Gerald Regan's, 6 but, the report said, it was thought that the acquisition of the steel plant might boost the new premier's chances.

Winston became aware of a heavily breathing presence behind him. On turning, he saw that the large lady was looking at the newspaper over his shoulder.

"Excuse me. May I help you?"

"You don't want to be payin' no mind to what that says," said the woman, whom he had seen—and heard—earlier. "Them taking over the plant may be some poplar here, but on the mainland they'll be giving him kick up the arse for puttin' money into Cape Breton."

"You must be Kenny's mother."

"That I am. How'd you know that?"

"Kenny described you to me. He told me to come here."

"I'll give him somethin' to describe when I gets him home! How was your breffast?"

"Good, thanks. Could you tell me please how I would get from here to Xavier College?"

"Sure can." She parked her considerable bulk across from him and on the table mat she drew a map which Winston seriously doubted would ever guide him to his destination. "I'm Gertie, by the way."

Winston paid his bill, regained his car and, peering at the scrawls on the map, gingerly poked the vehicle out into King's Road.

9

In the Hub, Alex MacDonald sat on his front steps, quietly smoking a roll-up made from a Vogue cigarette paper and MacDonald's Export A tobacco. Occasionally, Alex would allow himself an Old Port cigar, but only rarely, when he played cards with some friends who lived in New Aberdeen near Number 20 colliery.

Looking up the row, he could see Fred Butts, the mailman, on his rounds, a big, bulging sack banging against his side. Alex waved to him and Freddie waved back with his free arm.

His cigarette now finished, Alex ground the stub into the soil by the step with his heel, got up and strolled to the gate.

It was a poor, grey, rickety, wooden affair barely supported by ancient, rusted hinges. On either side of the gate were fence posts but no fence, their having long since collapsed. The remnants of the chicken wire which had once been strung between the posts could be seen poking through the soil at one end of the forecourt. The MacDonalds' front garden possessed nothing which legitimately entitled it to the name, as it was just a small, bare plot of scuffed-up earth sporting a few, sad tufts of grass.

By the time Alex had reached the gate, Fred Butts had delivered to the nearby houses and drew level with him.

"Good day, Freddie."

"Good day, Alec. How's she goin', b'y?"

"Good, b'y. What you got there for us?"

"Your Ma's pension cheque, and the light bill for you. But I got a bunch of stuff for next door."

"Let me have it, Freddie. I'll put it through their door. Save you the walk."

"Okay by me, b'y," said Fred, handing him a bundle of letters. "See you later."

"Not if I see you first!"

As he watched Fred disappear around the corner, he stuffed his mail into his back pocket and carried the McNeils' bundle back to the step. Once there, he leaned over to stuff it through the letter-box, when the door suddenly opened and he was brought face to face with Rita.

They were both startled, and Alex leapt back, his face reddened. Transfixed, he stared at her for a few seconds. Then they both laughed nervously.

"Oh, it's you, Alec."

"Yeah. Sorry 'bout that, Rita. I was just puttin' your mail through."

"Ah."

"Y'know, to save Freddie the walk, like."

"Right."

"Here you go," he said, handing her the mail.

"Thanks, Alec." She took the bundle from him, but lingered on the step.

"Oh, Rita?"

"Yes, Alec?"

He stopped, wondering if it would be today that he finally would summon up the strength and courage to say what was on his mind. He resolved to ask her to go out with him that evening, then imme-diately thought that would be too pushy. Maybe he would just ask if she wanted to walk with him to the edge of the cliff and look at the sea.

Rita looked at him quizzically, and he lost his nerve.

"Looks like it's goin' to be a great day, don't it?"

When Rita looked up at the sky in order to judge the validity of Alex's prediction, she offered a glimpse of herself which few might notice. But Alex did. He had seen it for a long, lonely time. It was an indication that she was not really as old or as dowdy as she at first appeared. He imagined her in a white wedding dress and was almost overcome by the vision.

"Yes. Looks pretty good," she said.

Alex nodded. He looked at her in silence. She looked back.

"Well," she said, breaking the spell, "I'd best go in..."

"Yeah."

"Y'know, take the letters...get the kettle on...make a bit of breffast."

"Yeah. Sorry to keep you, Rita."

"Thanks again, Alec. See you later."

"Not if I see you first."

They both laughed, but it was a forced formula, designed to end an awkwardness.

Rita went inside, closing the door behind her. She caught a corner of her apron in the door and had to reopen it. They laughed again and she disappeared.

Alex sat heavily on his step, sighing deeply. He sank into a pensive repetition of all-too-familiar speculations and wasted opportunities.

10

When Rita opened the kitchen door she found her mother, Katie, pottering about here and there. She seemed a little lost.

"'Mornin', Ma. You're up."

"Yeah. The time's getting on."

"What you looking for?"

"'Mornin', Rita. The kettle. Where's it at?"

"Right in front of you."

"Oh, so it is. I must have left me glasses upstairs."

"No, you got them on your nose."

"Oh, yeah." The old woman put her hand up and felt the spectacles. It was a very white, very pudgy, very blotched hand. Her engagement and wedding rings could scarcely be seen as the flesh had grown over them. If for any reason they needed to be removed, they would have to be cut off.

"Me eyes ain't what they used to be, girl," said Katie.

"You'd better get 'em checked out, Ma."

"I will, one day," said the old lady as she shuffled to the kettle.

Murdoch's snoring interrupted their conversation with sudden violence.

"My Jesus. He's kicking up one hell of a storm up there."

"Is he ever!" Rita said, involuntarily looking up. She imagined she could see where her father's loud grunting was shaking the light which hung from the ceiling.

"Y'know, I been married to that man for fifty-three years and it's never been any different," Katie said wistfully. "He can snore his head off all night and it don't bother me a bit, but once the sun is up it drives me crazy. I can doze a bit here and there, but I can't get no real sleep." She stared at her daughter. "You goin' to work? You best smarten yourself up fast, girl."

"I'm on the afternoon shift today."

"Oh yeah? What's that you got in your hand?"

"The mail. Alec just give it to me."

"What's Alec doin' with our mail? Don't he get enough mail of his own?"

"He got it from Freddie at the gate and brought it to me," Rita said with a laugh.

"Seems to me that feller's paying you a lot of attention that ain't called for."

"Ma!" Rita blushed. "What'n the Jesus are you talking about?"

"Hmm." The old woman pursed her lips, and murmured, "I know what I know." Louder, she said, "What's in the mail, anyways?"

"The usual stuff. Bills and that. And a letter from T'rono. Looks like our Dotty's handwriting."

"I wish you wouldn't call her Dotty, Rita. Gimme the letter!"

As Katie opened the letter, the kettle started whistling. Rita walked over and took it off the stove.

"You making the tea?"

"'Course I am, Ma. What'd you think I was doin?"

"Make it good and strong, girl. You know your father likes it black as Toby's arse."

Pulling her shabby robe around her, Rita put five teabags in the pot and poured the boiling water over them.

"Well?"

"Well, what?"

"Is it from our Dotty?"

"Yes," her mother said with a wince. "It's from Dorothy, alright."

"What's she got to say?"

"Oh, this and that."

"More boastin' about how her and Jeff is rollin' in money?"

"Rita!" Katie looked up. "You knows I don't like you talking like that. Dorothy's done right well for herself. There's nothing wrong in that. And I don't care what you say, she's got a good heart, And so's Jeff. He's a good provider."

"Kind of boring, though. All them grey suits and stiff shirts. And all that fancy talk about markets and interest rates."

Secretly, Rita was quietly jealous of her sister, but would never give her mother the satisfaction of knowing it. "What is he anyways, a banker?"

"He's a financial adviser."

"Who's he advisin'?"

"Clients."

"Clients! Sounds fishy to me."

"You don't know the first thing 'bout it, so shut your mouth and keep your nose out. It's better to be steady than full of flash and for sure better than bein' on pogey. He's made sure them kids never wanted for nothing.'"

"Yeah, I guess so," Rita conceded.

"I imagine you do! If only you had found a feller like Jeff, I wouldn't have to be worryin' 'bout you."

"Don't you worry 'bout me, Ma. I can take care of meself."

"Is that so? Well, I'm glad to hear it. You may have to take care of yourself soon enough, my girl."

"And what'n the Jesus does that mean?"

"Don't be usin' that coarse language with me, Rita. It's no wonder you couldn't get yourself a man."

Rita rolled her eyes and sighed. She had been here before innumerable times, and knew there was no sense to be made of an argument with her mother about men. Katie seemed to regard men as commodities which you chose, with no particular qualms about personal qualities, for convenience and security. She supposed that, if asked about her selection of Murdoch and their relationship, her mother would likely say there were worse men around than her husband and that they rubbed along well enough. That was quite contrary to Rita's ideas. She had been holding out for something called 'love' all these years and, although she guessed she would never find it, she knew she had been right to wait before getting wed.

"So tell me what's our Dotty got to say? You been clutching that there letter like it's a telegram from the Queen of England."

"Her and Jeff is moving into a new house. A much bigger one, she says."

"So?"

"She wants your father and me to go live with them."

"In T'rono? Jesus!" Rita exclaimed as Katie grimaced at her daughter's profanity. "And how does that idea grab you?"

"It grabs me fine, girl. Sounds pretty good after bein' stuck around this dirty old place for all these years."

"Hmm. Well good luck with the old man. It'll take some fast footwork and a load of honey to talk him into it."

"You're right there," said her mother, poking Rita in the chest with her finger. "But see here, Rita, let me do this in me own way and in me own time. Don't be sticking your oar in. If you can't back me on this, keep your mouth shut!"

"Whatever you say, Ma. Me gob's sealed tight as me arse."

"Huh! That'd be the first time, then!"

11

Winston Barber slowly, carefully, somewhat fearfully negotiated his way through the streets of Sydney. After New York City, this place had something of the air of a grown-up frontier town in a western movie. He found the road and street signs confusing and the traffic sometimes strange.

On what the sign told him was Townsend Street, a car in front of him suddenly stopped, and the driver proceeded to have a conversation out of his window with a man in a truck coming in the opposite direction. Winston waited patiently until they were finished and the driver of the truck had given him a cheery wave, and he drove on.

It became apparent that Kenny's mother's map was none too accurate, and he overshot the turning to George Street and carried on until he came to Prince Street, where he turned back toward the city centre, finally rediscovering George Street, where he drove, even more slowly, into the North End. Here, in a large, old building called The Lyceum, was the college or, from various signs, he deduced that it was part of college, other sections being scattered about. He found a parking spot on a side street, walked back and into a building in which time seemed to have stood still.

He had received garbled information on the telephone when he had called the college a week ago, and had been told to go to the college library to meet Professor Beaton. He warily put his head around the door and, apart from row upon row of books, saw only an elderly nun sitting at a desk.

"Come in, come in," she said. "You must be Mr. Barber."

"Good morning, Sister. I was told I would be seeing Professor Beaton."

"That's me!" said the old lady with glee. "By rights you should address me as Mother Saint Margaret of Scotland, but Sister Margaret will do."

Winston's prospective interlocutor was, he guessed, in her late seventies, was very small, thin and white with large spectacles, and wore a black coif over her head and a long serge habit to match.

"Sit ye down," she said. "How may I help you?"

Winston explained his mission, and that he was looking for background on the coal mining industry in Cape Breton, with particular reference to union activity.

"Well, young man, you have come to the right place, but whether we will have the time to do much more than adumbrate the general subject is doubtful." Sister Margaret indicated a pile of books on the desk in front of her. "Anticipating your arrival, I have assembled a few works which will give you the flavor of the topic."

"That's extremely kind of you, Sister," said Winston, putting his head on one side so he could see the titles. He saw *Miners and Steelworkers in Cape Breton, Blood on the Coal, Margaret's Museum*, and *Black Around the Eyes*, which sat on top of a number of typed essays.

"As you will see, our colourful mining history has occupied minds other than your own."

"I'm sure they will be very useful. Again, thank you."

"Is there any particular aspect which attracts you?"

"I'm doing this for Daniel Petrie, whom you may know—"

"Of course, a Glace Bay boy. He's made quite a name for himself in Hollywood."

"Yes. He asked me to take a general look, but said the 1925

strike would probably be the best focus."

"Ah, the 1925 strike! I remember it well. Not that I was living here then. I was in the seminary in Montreal, but my family--they were up in Inverness County—wrote and told me of the privation and confrontation." The old woman stared off into the distance. "I would have been…let me see… thirty-two at the time."

"It must have been horrific for the people who lived here in Sydney."

"Oh yes, and worse for those in Glace Bay and New Waterford. I think it might be fair to say that as many as 50,000 people were brought to the brink of starvation."

"Really?"

"Yes. Troops were sent in and even a warship from the navy."

"Wow. Who won in the end?"

"What do you mean?"

"The union or the mining company?"

"Oh, I see. Well, nobody really wins a battle of that nature. If any-one won in 1925 it was certainly the company. The men still had to take a cut in pay, and several of the collieries were closed, so un-employment increased."

"On that sobering note, I shall leave you."

Winston rose and picked up the books and papers. "And thanks again, Sister. Oh, how do I get to Glace Bay from here?"

"Go back up George Street, turn left on Prince and follow that road all the way there. It's about fifteen miles."

12

Wearing battered old slippers, green work pants, and a once-white tee shirt, Murdoch MacNeil sat eating his breakfast of baloney, bread and black tea, and reading the newspaper more voraciously than he devoured the food.

At the sink, Katie scrubbed and scoured a pot considerably longer and more vigorously than was necessary. Her being unable to think of a way to advantageously raise with Murdoch the subject dear to her heart, annoyed her, and led to her making rather more banging and clanging than usual.

At each resonant, metallic noise, her husband winced, but would not give her the satisfaction of inquiring the reason for her agitation. His motto was that, even when dogs were not sleeping, they should be allowed to lie undisturbed, for no matter how perturbing current circumstances might be, a far worse situation invariably lay in wait around the corner.

In a built-on porch at the rear of the house, Rita put clothes into an old dryer. When she closed the door and switched it on, it pulsated, rattled and groaned. Now dressed for the day, Rita wore flat shoes, a long brown skirt, and a yellowing white blouse under an old brown cardigan.

As she worked, she day-dreamed, as she often did, of a different kind of life. On some days the dream had her as a successful, independent woman—she never could decide as to what profession she belonged to—traveling the world, attending high-level meetings and conferences. On other days, she was the mistress of her own house, a nice house, a big house, out on Main Street towards Bridgeport. Her husband and children were never present in these dreams, but she knew they existed and were not far away. The outside of the house was a nice, dove grey—like Manning Macintyre's house—with white trim. The lush lawn was smooth and bottle green. Inside, the walls were beige, the furniture—from Cunningham's in Sydney—in cream and dark brown, and the thick, luxurious carpet was a rich burgundy.

Her mother's voice, surprisingly harsh and loud emanating from such a small person, roused Rita from her reverie.

"Always washin'. Always cleanin'. It's so dirty around here, there's no end to it. Dirt everywhere!"

Rita smiled to herself. She instantly recognized that this was the beginning of a protracted performance designed to sweeten Murdoch for the bitter pill her mother undoubtedly wished to subsequently administer to him.

"I used to think that when some of the pits closed around here it might get a little bit cleaner, but it's just as bad as ever it was. For the life of me I don't know where all the dirt comes from."

"It's no dirtier here than anywhere else," Murdoch growled, not looking up from his *Cape Breton Post*. "You don't know what you're talking about, woman."

"That's just it, ain't it? The whole place is filthy! Dirty old town!"

"*I met my love by the gas works wall,*" Rita sang in a low voice as she folded some laundry. "*Dreamed a dream by the old canal. I kissed my man by the factory wall. Dirty old town. Dirty old town.*"

"And just listen to that wind," said Katie, savagely glaring at Rita. "Even on a beautiful day like this, you can't get away from it. Day and night. Wind, wind, wind. It right wears you down."

"It's not the only thing that wears you down," Rita muttered under her breath.

"What's that?"

"I said, we gets the wind because we lives near the sea."

"The sea! I should've thought we'd all had quite enough of that old sea by now. I don't know what good it's ever done for us."

"Oh, I don't know, Ma. It's nice to look at now and then."

"By the jumpins!" Katie glared at Rita, this time with more venom. "I don't know how we put up with that stupid sea and that God-forsaken wind all them years! We must've been crazy!"

"Fresh air. That's what it is," muttered Murdoch, still glued to his newspaper. "Healthy, fresh air. It's good for your health."

"Health, my arse!" Katie spat and glowered at her husband. Then, with something between a grunt and a roar, she turned back to the sink and, with enhanced volume. bashed the frying pan against a saucepan with such force it left a small dent. She turned to Rita with a snarl. "As for you, my girl, you better get them clothes hung and drying. Right quick!"

"Yes, Ma," Rita replied meekly, gathered up armfuls of laundry, stuffed them into a large basket and headed out to the yard.

The back areas of the two adjoining company houses were separated by a low, flimsy fence, part of it made from wooden slats, part from chicken wire. At the end of the yards was a more substantial board fence, partially screening them from a narrow ginnel or passageway which ran between theirs and the backyards of the houses on the next street.

The MacNeils' yard was little more than a plot comprising a strip of cracked concrete next to the house, and a larger patch of scrubby, untended grass, which passed for a lawn, on which were scattered a weather-beaten old table and three aluminum chairs. Running from the roof of the porch to the board fence was a yellow plastic line, propped up in the middle by a tall, leaning pole. On this line, Rita started to affix her washing with colourful pegs.

Next door, the MacDonalds had a smaller, but better-kept, lawn near the house, and beyond it was a stretch of earth which Alex liked to call his garden, although he recognized that the description was somewhat flattering to his less than successful efforts. A few of his lonely flowers and sparse crops were clinging to life, but most looked seriously fatigued and undernourished and appeared as if they were ready to succumb. Alex crouched down by his spindly tomato plants—seven in number—and pulled up the weeds which were clearly thriving more heartily than the crop.

When he saw Rita coming out with her laundry, he edged back behind the leafy plants and stared, adoringly, longingly, at her. As Rita bent down to the basket, her cardigan fell open, and it became apparent that under her dowdy disguise, she was an extremely shapely woman. Alex, who had watched her many, many times, already knew this about Rita, but he could not see it too often.

To attract her attention, he cleared his throat and started to hum *A Bridge over Troubled Water,* which had been playing, almost incessantly, on radio since the beginning of the year. Hearing him, Rita strolled to the fence and looked over.

"Oh, it's you, Alec. I didn't know you were there, b'y."

"Hi, there, Rita. I was just weedin' my tomaters."

"They're looking a tad sad."

"Yeah, I know. The dirt around here is just useless," Alex said, rising and walking over to the fence. He wondered if he dared lean on it, which would bring his face close to hers, but decided against the move. "There's too much coal dust in the soil. I gotta get some fertilizer on them."

"They needs somethin'."

"Looks like Katie got you hard at work, girl."

"I hadda get outta the house. We got ourselves a situation today."

"How's that?"

"Ma got a letter from our Dotty. Says she wants Ma and Daddy to go live with them in Ontario."

"Jeez. I can't see Murdoch goin' for that."

"Me neither. He don't know about it yet. That's what's causing the situation. Ma's skating all around it."

"I don't bet she can keep that up for long."

"I don't know when she plans to drop the bomb, but whenever she does, he's the one goin' to explode."

"Tricky."

"You got that right. Look, Alec, when he finds out, like as not he'll come moaning to you, so for Chrissakes don't let on you knows anything about it."

"Fair enough, Rita."

"Thanks, Alec." Rita said, stopping down and picking up her basket. She made to go when Alex spoke again.

"Er, Rita?"

"Yeah."

"You…er…got any big plans for tonight?" There he'd said it. He held his breath.

"I'm workin', b'y. On the afternoon shift."

"Oh right. 'Course you are. I should've known."

"Well, I'll see you Alec."

"Yeah, see you, Rita."

She did not seem to notice, but his voice was inexpressibly sad. He watched her go back into the house and it was several minutes before he turned back to his weeding.

13

Sometime in the late 1800s, Senator William McDonald, who was born in 1837 in Inverness County, erected a collection of adjoining buildings at the intersection of Commercial, Main and Union streets in Glace Bay. Forever after, this was known as Senator's Corner, the scene of many stirring events such as mass gatherings, in addition to some less than reputable occurrences, most involving the overuse of alcohol. In the past, fights had been common here and at least one murder had taken place.

A large red brick edifice, The Glace Bay Hotel, occupied the triangle between Union and Main streets, and contained a spacious restaurant presided over by a quiet, elderly Chinese gentleman named George, and a tiny, very loud, shrew of a woman, known to all as Winnie. In the kitchen, and seldom seen in the restaurant, was Eddie the cook.

What their real Chinese names were, nobody knew and, just when they, or their forebears, had relocated from China to Cape Breton was known only to them. They supported a large extended family of over thirty people, most living in the immediate neighbourhood. When they all got together for Chinese New Year, the hotel was closed to the public and became the scene of a riotous celebration in which each celebrant was given his or her own bottle of Queen Anne whisky to drink with dinner.

On Union Street, next to the hotel, was a small, rather run-down book store owned by a self-confessed Communist, Norman

Lipchitz. Nobody quite knew how this business continued to operate, since its wares were largely unattractive and trade never appeared to be brisk. However, Norman himself was always prepared for an esoteric discussion on the theory of surplus value or the importance of heightening the contradiction, with any who felt themselves sufficiently informed and had several hours to spare.

In the triangle between Union and Commercial Streets there were several businesses, including a barber's shop, a small clothing store—Tiptop Tailors—and the Melody Café. The café belonged to Annie Pyke, and she ruled over her domain with a rod of iron, tempered by kindness and an understanding of the frailties of human nature.

The Melody was like a thousand other small restaurants the world over, spotlessly clean and shining with plastic and chrome. The table tops were finished with Formica, a substance heralded as a miracle when it came out about a decade before and, though a little faded now, was still serviceable.

Annie, having wiped the furniture clean, laid each table with cutlery, filled the napkin dispensers, and checked the salt, pepper and ketchup, stood in the doorway and surveyed the street.

"Good Morning, Mr. Fergusson," she called to a very tall man in his early sixties.

"Good morning, Miss Pyke." He was dignified and soft-spoken, but always looked a little lost.

"I guess the legislature is not sitting now?"

"No, indeed. We've risen for the summer."

Neil Layton Fergusson was a moderately-successful lawyer who had been elected to the legislature fourteen years previously, and re-elected three times since then, largely, it was said, because he was a nice man and had been an outstanding baseball player.

"Risen? Like the good Lord?"

"No, no, I meant adjourned. Risen is just a term we use."

"I know," Annie said with a laugh. "I was just teasin' you."

"Ah. Well, good day to you."

She watched him cross Commercial Street, then Main Street, and go into his office, which was next to a funeral parlour.

Just then, Marlene MacKinnon, the first of her two staff members, arrived in a flutter, not about being late—she was never that—but about not being early. Marlene was a wispy little mouse of sixteen who was invariably worried, always apologetic, and constantly on the verge of tears. Annie felt sorry for her, but never showed it because she believed that if she gave her staff an inch they would take a mile, and Annie had no intention of allowing that to happen.

"'Mornin', Marlene. I done pretty much everything already. You get changed and straighten the chairs out," Annie said, knowing that the chairs were perfectly straight, but she also knew that the Devil found work for idle hands.

"Good morning, Annie." A rich, booming, but mellow voice came from a bouncy figure who had come down Main Street and was about to go into the hotel.

"Hello, Leo," Annie called to Leo MacIntyre, another lawyer, of the opposite political persuasion from Layton Fergusson, whose speciality was as a public speaker at dinners, weddings, and any other events which called for lengthy, orotund addresses, lofty tones and carefully tailored anecdotes.

"Any luck yet?" she asked, having heard the rumour that Leo was trying to get an appointment as a Provincial Court judge.

"No, sadly not." As Leo shook his head, his sloping forehead gleamed in the sunlight. "I think I shall have to wait until my party gets in, although goodness knows when that will be."

"You're not impressed with Mr. Regan, then?" She referred to the forty-two-year-old Leader of the Opposition, who had been chosen by his party a few years earlier.

"Oh, I wouldn't say that, Annie," said Leo hastily. "I think he put on a splendid performance last year."

"You mean that—waddyacallit—filibuster. How long did he go on for?"

"Fifteen hours. Extraordinary. I think it made a favourable impression, but the Conservatives have been in office for a long time and seem to be entrenched." Leo paused. "I imagine you vote the same way as your father."

"Daddy always voted labour. CCF and NDP and always will, but I got a mind of me own, Leo."

"I'm glad to hear it. Well, I must go. I have to be in court in Sydney in an hour."

Annie went to the corner, peeked up Union Street and saw Gloria Maddin, her second staff member, hurrying down the street. Gloria was everything Marlene was not. She was a voluptuous, twenty-year-old, peroxide blonde who oozed sexuality. She was as scantily clad as Annie would let her get away with, and shamelessly flaunted her physical attributes.

"Sorry I'm late, Annie. Me Ma didn't set the alarm clock."

"Is that so?" Annie said sternly. "Neither you nor your Ma live up this street. You lives on the other side of town."

"I...er..."

"D'you go home last night?"

"Well..."

"Get inside," Annie snapped.

With her staff, she pretended to be more straight-laced than she really was, and while she felt obliged to adopt a high moral tone with Gloria, she was secretly jealous of her escapades.

Making a show of shaking her head, she herded Gloria into the café and followed her in.

14

In the Melody Café, all three women were awaiting the arrival of customers, so, as usual, all were looking out at the town to see who was going where, and guessing for what purposes they were on the move.

They watched as Peter Borsato, dressed to the nines in a smart, but old fashioned, green suit and a white Stetson, passed on the first of a number of perambulations through the town. He had almost completed this morning's exercise and was returning to his lodgings at Jennie Jones's boarding house on Minto Street. He walked with difficulty because he had Lymphedema, blockages in his lymphatic system, requiring him to wear bell-bottomed trousers.

Peter's story was not dissimilar from those of a number of immigrants who had come from Italy, Poland, and Russia to work in the Cape Breton coal mines many years ago. They worked hard, but made few friends, spoke only rudimentary English, and remained unmarried all their lives. Alexandr Kuznetsovich, for example, had evacuated from Odessa on a ship barely an hour before Trotsky's Red Army arrived to sack the city after the end of World War I. He went from pillar to post, eventually landing in Sydney by accident rather than design.

Peter Borsato was originally from Genova, where at the age of 20 he fell in love with the daughter of a rich don. She loved him, too, but the father would have none of him because he was poor, and as a result she rejected him. Heartbroken he wandered down to the docks and boarded the first ship which was leaving port. He, too, found himself in Cape Breton, where he spent the rest of his life.

Annie and her staff also saw Bunny "Me" McKenzie loping up the sidewalk. When Marlene waved to him, he crossed the now-busy street and came into the restaurant.

"'Lo, Annie, 'lo, Gloria, 'lo, Marlene."

"Good morning, Bunny," said Annie. "Where are you off to?"

"Me goes everywhere, b'y," said Bunny in an almost strangulated voice. "Me goes to the post office, then me goes to the wharf."

"And I guess you'll be havin' a high time tonight in Iggy's tavern?"

"No, b'y! Me goin' to bingo tonight. Me likes bingo. Me be's there all the time, b'y."

As Bunny turned out of the door, Winston Barber's sports car went slowly, throatily, past, looking for a parking space.

"You see that?" exclaimed Gloria.

"What?" Marlene asked.

"New York plates."

"Yeah," said Annie. "Don't get many of them."

"Maybe it's him," Marlene ventured.

"Who?"

"The movie man. I heard tell a feller is comin' from Hollywood about that movie they was talkin' about in the *Post Record*."

The two local newspapers, *The Post* and *The Record,* had merged to become the *Cape Breton Post* fourteen years ago, but most people still referred to it by its former masthead.

"Ooh," Gloria said, "I heard 'bout that. D'you think that's him?"

"He's parked in front of Borden's store," said Annie from the door.

"Where's he heading?" Gloria asked.

""Hush, the pair of you! I think he's comin' here."

Winston gingerly opened the door, peered in and smiled. While it would be an exaggeration, if not a distortion of the truth, to say that three hearts were broken in that moment, three hearts certainly did beat faster, accompanied by a degree of accelerated breathing.

"Are you open?"

"Oh yes," Annie said quickly, thinking the unsayable, and indicated a table in the window. "You come on in and sit right over there."

Winston ambled over to the table, sat down and stretched out his long legs. Both Gloria and Marlene dashed across the room to wait on him, but Annie rapidly moved into the space between them and their target and blocked their way.

"It's alright, girls, I'll take care of this," she snapped like a garter belt. "Marlene, get some more french fries out of the freezer. Gloria, you go out and clean the front window."

Sulking, the girls moved away and set about their apportioned tasks. Annie swept her hair from her ear and pulled her apron a little tighter. A surge of norepinephrine swept through her nervous system and she felt her stomach hot behind the butterflies which were fluttering there. She did not know precisely what was happening to her, but she knew she wanted this man, not forever, maybe, not even for a week, but she wanted him soon, and as down and dirty as it gets.

"Now then," she said, slightly out of breath, "what can I get you?"

"May I have a menu?"

"Sure." Annie stared at him but continued to clutch the menu.

"Please."

"Oh. Right. Sorry." She passed it to him.

"I don't need too much," he said.

I'd give you everything, Annie thought, but did not say.

"I had a huge breakfast in Sydney, so I think I'll just have a cup of coffee and some pie."

"Right."

"What can you offer me?" Winston asked.

Everything, thought Annie, but did not say. Aloud, she said "What?"

"What kinds of pie do you have?"

"Oh…er…apple. And cherry."

"I'll have the cherry," Winston said slowly.

Annie burned with blushes and, taking a deep breath, scurried away.

Her hands were shaking as she cut an extra-large piece of pie and placed it on a plate, but before taking it and the coffee to Winston, she paid a quick visit to the mirror in the back room to check if anything could be done to enhance her appearance.

While she was there, Gloria's face appeared outside the front window and, making circular motions with a wet chamois, gaped at Winston through the glass. He noticed her, looked up and flashed a smile. Gloria beamed and gave him a little wave with the chamois.

Regretfully concluding that she could do nothing to make herself more desirable in the time available, Annie rushed out of the back room, grabbed the plate and cup and returned to Winston's table. She put the plate and coffee in front of him and glared at Gloria.

"Don't pay no mind to her. You know what these young girls are like."

"What are they like?"

"Oh, loud and lucky, but they don't know what they're doin' half the time. They don't got the experience." She blushed again.

"She's not bothering me. Besides, you're not much older yourself."

"Not in years, maybe." Annie could not believe what she was saying or why she was saying it, and quickly changed tack. "To be honest, mister, I got ten tears on that one outside."

All this while, Gloria was slowly, meticulously, cleaning every last square inch of the window in an effort to prolong her ringside view. Annie slid into the booth across from Winston.

"Well, you don't look it," he said.

"Thank, b'y." Annie responded, flustered anew. "I'm Annie."

"Pleased to meet you, Annie, I'm Winston."

"Them girls think you're the movie man."

"The movie man?" Winston smiled broadly.

"Yeah, they seen the plates on your car and figured you was the one mentioned in the *Post Record* about coming up here to see about doin' another movie."

"There have been other movies made here?"

"Yeah, a few. You don't mind me joining you?"

"Not at all."

"I'll get meself a coffee. You want a top-up?"

"Sure. Thank you."

Annie went back to the counter and grabbed a pot off the ring.

Before she could return to the table, Marlene silently sidled up to her. "Is it him?"

"Don't be doin' that. You scares the life outta me, creepin' around."

"Sorry. But is it him?"

"Shush. I haven't found out yet. But I will."

Back at the table, Annie put the pot between her and Winston and sat down. As she sat down, she slipped the engagement ring off her hand and put it in her apron pocket.

"So, tell me. Are you the movie man?"

"I guess I am the movie man, yes."

15

While Annie and Winston were drinking coffee, Gloria, knowing when she was temporarily beaten, moved on to other sections of the window. Since there was no motive for her to be meticulous here, she gave these only cursory attention and finally tired of the work. She threw the chamois into the bucket, edged just beyond Annie's eye line, leaned against the wall, and took out a cigarette.

As she puffed on her du Maurier, she pulled back her shoulders and pushed forward so as to display her ample breasts to even better advantage. The number of calls and whistles from passing boys and men indicated that the ploy had achieved its desired result.

"Lookin' good, Glore," hollered Fred Binder.

"I wishes I could say the same for you, Freddie!"

"You should've seen me when I was younger, girl."

"Reckon that'd be before me Ma's time!" Gloria cackled.

Gloria Maddin had always been considered something of a tear-away among her family members, and by a far less flattering term in the wider population of Glace Bay. It was said that she "got it from her mother" because Valerie Maddin was something of a good-time girl after her husband, Jim, was killed in Number Twenty pit when Gloria was only nine. Less charitable people said Valerie's wild ways went back even further, but all agreed that Gloria never had much of a chance with a mother like Val.

Valerie had a job as a cleaner at St. Joseph's Hospital, at which she was fairly conscientious, but as soon after she got home from work (and often she did not wait until then), she could be found in one of the taverns, legions or clubs. Her favourite place was the Army and Navy Club on Minto Street—popularly known as "the swinging tit"—where she would drink and gossip with Bill Talbot, Ollie Barrett or Buddy MacEachern. This usually meant that when the young Gloria got home from school, she would get her own, not very nutritious, meal and watch television. Just as often she would go to bed before Valerie returned to the house. Sometimes she did not return, and Gloria had to arrange her own breakfast and get off to school the next day in a disheveled state.

A man Gloria called "Uncle Lauchie" used to come to the house to "keep company" with Val, and when he did not find her home he took a shine to her daughter. But Gloria did not continue her relationship with Uncle Lauchie for very long, having found him too old, too smelly, and too cheap for her new tastes.

Thus liberated, she cast her bread upon the waters and found that her kindness was reciprocated in many ways by many men.

"Good day, Gloria," said a handsome lad of about eighteen, riding a bicycle. "How's she goin'?"

"Good, Randy. How's she goin' yourself?"

"Not three bad, girl. What's new?"

"Take a peek around the corner. Don't let her indoors see you—I said *don't* let her see you!"

"Alright, don't get your panties in a twist."

"I ain't got none on." Gloria giggled.

"Oh my Lord!" Randy said, pretending to faint. "I'll be thinkin' of that all day."

"Well do your thinkin' when you're gone, b'y. You see that feller in there with Annie."

"Yeah. So what?"

"Marlene reckons he's the feller that's come to see about makin' a movie here."

"What, here in Glace Bay?"

"That's what they're sayin'."

"Maybe he can get you in the movies."

"Oh sure, that's goin' to happen."

"You got the body for the movies, anyways, Gloria."

"Go 'way with you," she said, slapping him on the arm, and then pushing him away. "Don't be saucy!"

"Gotta go. See you."

"Not if I see you first."

Gloria watched Randy ride off and, satisfying herself that there was no longer an audience for her to entertain, returned to the window and, with one long swipe of the chamois, came back to the place where she could observe Annie and Winston.

They were still talking and drinking coffee, but Gloria noted with disapproval that their heads were closer together than they had previously been. She contrived to put her ear against the glass, but the conversation was only a faint burble.

Tired of this task, she grabbed the bucket and went back inside.

"What you want to do is to talk to some of the older fellers," Annie was saying, "They're full of all that union and strike stuff in the olden times. I shouldn't wonder if some of them was actually involved with it at the time."

"That's exactly what I had in mind," said Winston. "Would you be able to give me names of men I could go to see?"

"Sure. My old man would be a good one, for starters. His name is Art Pyke, You'll find him down The Hub."

"The Hub?"

"Yeah, that's the lower part of New Aberdeen, or Number Two as we calls it."

"Why?"

"Why what?"

"Why do you call in Number Two?"

"'Cause the colliery that's there now—Number Twenty—is on top of where Number Two used to be. I think they used the same shafts as Number Two."

"When did this Number Two close?"

"Way back. When I was a baby, I guess. I heard dad say that Number Two was one of the largest collieries in the world. He said they got 30 million tons out of it,"

"That's a lot of coal. I imagine it was a dangerous business working there."

"Oh yeah. Before I was born, dad said there was a big bump that killed four miners."

"What's a bump?"

"You'd have to ask someone who knows more than me, but as far as I know it's not exactly an explosion, but like a volcano underground."

"What about the mine which came later—Number Twenty. Any accidents there?"

"Listen, b'y, there's always accidents in these mines. When I was a little girl, there was a big explosion in Number Twenty which killed seven fellers. Gas, it was, me Dad said."

"Wow!"

"They brought in a new law after that did away with the shot-firers wearing head lamps. They hadda use safety lamps."

"Shot firers? These are the men who set the explosives?"

"Yeah. Listen, I ain;'t never been in a mine in me life, b'y. You're talking to the wrong person if you wants the ins and the outs of it."

"Okay," said Winston, draining the coffee pot into his cup. "Who is the right person?"

"Any one of a dozen or more. You'd likely find most of them down the Pensioners' Union. That's just over on Main Street. You can see it from here." Annie pointed to an old, rather run-down house.

"Who would I ask for?"

"If Dad is there, ask for Art Pyke. Or Archie the Buck…"

"Archie the Buck?"

'Yeah. Archie MacIntyre. They calls him 'the buck' 'cause he's right buckish."

"I don't understand. What's 'buckish'?"

"Haha. That's what we call people from the country. Like from Inverness or Victoria counties. They've got a bit of a lisp when they talks. I guess it comes from the Gaelic. There's a lot in the country that still speaks Gaelic, you know."

"Really?' He took a sip of his coffee. "Who else should I look for?"

"Billy Pitman, Danny the Dancer MacDonald, Murdoch Matheson, and Russell MacPhee, but I don't think they'll be there until around two or three this afternoon."

"That's a bit of a wait," said Winston, consulting his watch. "But thanks, anyway." He jotted down the names she had given him into a small notebook.

"Tell you what," Annie exclaimed. "I just thought of it! You should go see Bright Alec. He's up in The Hub, too."

"Bright Alec?"

"Yeah. Alec MacDonald. They calls him 'Bright Alec' 'cause he's been around the world and is always readin' books."

"And he would be a good source for me?"

"Sure would. He's up on all that historical stuff and if he don't know somethin' he'll know somebody who does."

"He sounds like just the person I need. Where would I find him?"

"On Third Street. Look, go down Main Street—just over there— and turn left on Minto. Then go through The Stirling, that is you goes up Stirling Road 'till you hit Ryan Street. You got all that?"

"I think so," Winston said, writing furiously.

"At the end of Ryan Street you're in The Hub. Just ask anyone there for Bright Alec."

"Thank you so much Annie," he said, standing up and putting a five dollar bill on the table. "I don't know how to thank you."

I can think of a way. O can I ever! she thought, but did not say.

As she watched him go and returned to her duties behind the counter, she slipped her engagement ring out of her pocket and back onto her finger.

16

Donnie MacNeil and a group of miners squatted on the ground in the main deep, having their lunch. Scattered around them were lunch boxes, lamps and work gloves. On the outskirts of their seated circle, a small army of rats looked eagerly on, hoping for leftovers when the meal was finished. One lucky rat was actually being fed crusts of bread by Harvey MacDonald, a disheveled miner who sat slightly apart from the others.

"Come on then, John F. Have another little bite," Harvey said to the nibbling creature.

"Don't be encouraging them, Harvey," said Will MacPherson, a miner from Bridgeport. "If you feeds him, more'll come and we'll never get any peace."

"Mind your own fuckin' business," Harvey retorted.

"Alright, take it easy. Why do you call that vermin John F., any-ways?"

"I named him after the fuckin' magistrate what fined me the other week."

"Up before the judge huh? What for?"

"The fuckin' missus said I laid a beatin' on her."

"Holy cow, your own missus had you up in court?" Gerald Tracey exclaimed.

"Yeah. The cow got up and told the fuckin' judge that I bet her at home a few times, then when I come back from the tavern I bet her again."

"And what did you say," asked Donnie.

"I said no pay no fuckin' mind to her, John F. She's fuckin' punch drunk. The bastard fined me fifty bucks."

"My heavens," interjected Chester MacLeod, "What would the good Lord say if he could hear the way you're going on?"

"Listen, Chester, there's things goin' on down in this here pit the good Lord don't know fuck all about!"

Not far away, a massive, gleaming Anderton shearer stood waiting to cut many more tons from the dark seam embedded in the slightly lighter coloured rock. This monster, invented by James Anderton in 1953, was a widely-used machine with a five-foot-diameter cutting drum, and had been successfully used throughout the British coalfields, producing some 70% of all coal mined there. The machine travelled on an armoured conveyor and sheared the coal in one direction, then returned along the face, loading the broken coal.

The only drawback of this highly efficient machine was that it could only be used where the coal seam was more than 3.5 feet thick, because use on a thin seam would create a large amount of fine coal dust and increase the permeability of the coal, allowing methane gas to escape into the mine atmosphere which would create a dangerous explosive hazard. This was not a problem in No. 20 colliery, where the Phalen seam was at least seven feet thick in most places.

"How's your Annie?" asked Will.

"Better'n nothing," Donnie said. They both laughed. "No, she's good, b'y."

"Jesus, Donnie b'y," said Will, "I don't know how you do it. You been gettin' regular tail from the same woman for pretty near five years, and she ain't managed to drag you to the altar yet."

"Not so regular," said Donnie, lowering his voice. "It ain't easy. I lives with me parents and sister, and she lives with her old man."

"Ah, I sees the problem."

"And it's kind of dear to go getting motel rooms."

"I guess it is. I should've thought that would give you more reason to get hitched with Annie."

Donnie grinned sheepishly and poked some coal dirt out of his eye with his just as dirty finger.

"What's this?" asked Gerald, scooching himself closer to them.

"Talking about me not being married."

"How long you been courtin'?"

"Five years."

"A friggin miracle, I'd call it."

"I'll do it eventually, b'y," Donnie said. "One of those days. I got nothin' against it. We just been waitin' til we could afford a house, but the prices is sky high."

"That's true," said Will. "I wouldn't want to be startin' out now with my Margie. The costs of furniture and stuff is ridiculous."

"I had a bad spell on the comp, and Annie had a lot of expenses when her mother died. And, like fools, we blew a lot on that trip to Disneyland."

"Yeah," Gerald said, "If you gotta get a house,even if you're rentin', you got to get a table, chairs, chesterfield, stove, fridge—"

"And a television. They ain't cheap." Will chipped in as Chester and Harvey moved over to their spot.

"And there's always the possibility of short time," Donnie said. "Actually, I could do with extra shifts if I could get them."

"I thinks you'd be better off the way you are, b'y. You got it pretty good, and not likely to get any better," Gerald said.

His light dancing along the walls, the overman walked along the deep. He shouted out at spaced intervals, "Five minutes, b'ys."

"Yeah, fuckin' yeah," Harvey snarled.

"Donnie, you getting' lucky tonight?" Chester asked.

"No, b'y. I'm goin' to be havin' a quiet time with the TV and a case of Tenpenny."

"Say, Donnie, what's with that sister of yours?" Harvey butted in.

"What sister? I got two of them."

"That Rita, The one that's livin' home. I never heard tell of her goin' out with any feller."

"I don't know," said Donnie, "I guess that's her business."

"She's not one of them lezzies, is she?"

"You're looking for a puck in the mouth, you know that?"

"Alright, alright, I'm only sayin'. I didn't mean anythin' by it."

The overman retraced his journey, this time carrying a pan shovel someone had left lying around. He rattled his yardstick against it.

The men hastily stuffed the last of their sandwiches into their mouths, got up, stretched and put on their gloves.

"Wait b'ys" said Chester, "I forgot to tell you. I heard they're going to close the pit."

"What pit?"

"This pit."

"No!"

"I heard one of the overmen saying something about it."

"What the fuck does he know, b'y?" Harvey growled.

"He knows a fuckin' sight more'n you do," Will snapped.

"That's all I'd need," lamented Donnie. "To lose me job at a time like this."

"Yeah." Harvey wiped his nose with his sooty hand. "Things is getting so fuckin' slow around here, the Mira River is only running three days a week."

17

Following Annie's directions, Winston was slowly threading his way through the streets when suddenly Lonnie Kelly lurched out of an alley and into the road. Winston stood on his brakes and the car screeched to a halt as Lonnie fell back into the gutter.

A few passers–by rushed to the scene, while some stationary gawkers behind their fences or their windows looked on.

Winston jumped out, ran round to where Lonnie was lying, and with the help of an older, semi-disabled man, tried to elevate him to an upright position.

Lonnie, red-eyed, reeling and dribbling, responded by loudly abusing his would-be helpers in language which, even in Cape Breton, would be considered violent.

"Are you alright, sir?" Winston asked solicitously.

"Leave me alone!" Lonnie bawled, fixing Winston in a fierce glare. He took a wild swing which Winston avoided by taking a quick step backwards. "Fuck off, you bastards!"

Breaking free, and swaying from side to side, Lonnie stumbled away up the street. Suddenly he stopped, turned round, and addressed them in a somewhat more civil tone.

"Say, either of you got any liquour on ya?" On seeing them shake their heads, he turned back and recommenced his shaky journey. "Fuck yez then!"

"Shouldn't we get him to a hospital or something?" Winston asked the other Samaritan, "isn't he hurt?"

"No, b'y. He fell before your car even got close to him. I seen the whole thing."

"Should we notify the police?"

"I wouldn't do that, b'y. They won't thank you for doin' it. My name's Bobby Hayes, by the way."

"Oh. Hi, Bobby. I'm Winston Barber."

"Pleased to meet you, Winston. You ain't from around here?"

"No, California by way of New York."

"Oh yeah, now I look I can see your number plates."

"Tell me why we shouldn't report him to the police?"

"'Cause that feller, Lonnie, is after fallin' down three times a day, every day of the week."

"Can't anyone do anything for him?"

"No, b'y. He's a lost cause. Best give him a wide berth. When he gets a real load on, he's after destroying all kinds of stuff."

"Really?"

"Yeah, winders, doors, and anythin' that ain't screwed down."

"Do they ever put him in prison?"

"Oh yeah, every now and again. He was in the County jail not long ago. He just got out a coupla days ago."

"Oh, I see."

"Problem was Lonnie got picked up right after he collected his welfare cheque."

"Why was that a problem?"

"It made him right cocky. See John F—"

'That's MacDonald the judge?"

"Right. You knows 'bout him, do you? Yeah, that's him. Anyways, John F. found him guilty and sentenced him to thirty dollars of a fine. So, right full of himself, Lonnie said, .That's alright, judge, I got that in me arse pocket.'"

"What did the judge say to that?"

"Wait now, b'y, I'm tellin' ya. So John F. Said, 'And a month in the

County jail. Let's see if you got that in your arse pocket!'"

They both laughed, whereupon Bobby said he had to go to town, and hobbled on down the street.

Winston drove on, but where Minto Street joined Sterling Road, he accidentally turned right onto Ocean Avenue, which in turn became Upper North Street, giving him a sudden, and unexpected, expansive view of the ocean. There were houses along the left hand side of the road, but for almost the entirety of North Street he could see none on the seaward side.

,Just before he reached the first sea-side house there was an extensive stretch of grass, so he pulled the car over to the verge, parked and got out.

Carefully, he stepped on to the grass and walked to the end of the cliff. Underfoot, the growth was soft and springy, and he could smell the savoury wild thyme and detect the fragrant, sweet partridge berry. It was a magnificent day, the wind was uncharacteristically soft, and there was nothing to obstruct his vision in any direction.

To his left, he could quite clearly see a rocky headland. He later discovered that this, part of the district known as Table Head, was where Guglielmo Marconi established his first permanent transatlantic wireless station, an historic event which started the age of global wireless communications.

To his far right, he could see the Schooner Pond promontory, and beyond that tiny Flint Island with its lighthouse.

Ahead, there was nothing but blue. The sea was a darker, but not deeper, blue than the sky. Perhaps the water was a slightly greyish blue, while the sky was a rich cobalt. But upon the sea's surface the light from the sky reflected in a trillion pinpoints, like diamonds, which dazzled the eyes and caused a sharp intake of the breath.

From a point just above the horizon, directly in front of him, pure white clouds, pockedmarked with blue, spread like a fan until they got lost in what he supposed was the stratosphere. In the air, quiet except for the tweeting of the birds and the faint 'chunking' from Number 26 Colliery a few miles away, Winston stood there and admired; one might even say 'worshipped', he thought.

"Great day, Mister."

The voice came from behind him. He turned round to see a tall, smiling, fresh-faced young man dressed in the uniform of the Salvation Army.

Winston walked over to him. "It is a very great day," he said. "I'm Winston Barber."

"I'm Butch Simmons. I live just down the road here. You new around here?"

"Yes, from New York."

"I seen that on your plates. On vacation or visiting family?"

"Neither really. I'm doing research."

"Research?"

"Yes, a friend of mind, Dan Petrie—"

"We knows him, alright. Been gone from here for some time now."

"I'm doing some work for him."

"Goin' to do a movie?"

"Maybe. Nothing is definite."

"Oh."

"Butch, could you tell me how I get to The Hub from here, please? I was supposed to get onto Sterling Road, but I got sidetracked,"

"Sure. You goes up here. Take a left on Roost Street, then a right, and that puts you back on Sterling Road."

"Thank you, very much." Winston shook hands with him and climbed back into his car.

"God bless you on your journey," Butch said, then added, "Keep me in mind for one of them extra jobs in the movie."

"I'll do my best."

"Hallelujah!" cried Butch as Winston drove off.

18

Murdoch MacNeil sat on an old, faded, brown, naugahyde couch which resembled himself in many respects, put his feet up on a battered ottoman (which Rita insisted on calling a 'pouf') and commenced to read the *Cape Breton Post* in a serious manner. He intended to read every last word of it, in order to keep himself fully occupied during what he sensed would be an extended period of his wife 'going on the warpath'.

Murdoch did not know precisely the size or species of bee in Katie's righteous bonnet today, but he knew there was an *apis* of some variety or other nesting there. From living half a century with her, he knew that when she started banging and crashing about the place it was in preparation for some kind of battle. Experience also told him that when this occurred, he was seldom the victor. While he knew a defeat of as yet unknown magnitude was inevitable in the future, he was resolved to postpone it as long as possible.

Passive resistance was his chosen weapon. When combined with carefully chosen sarcasm, Murdoch had found it reasonably effective, although he conceded that his wife could also wield it to good effect.

"Ach, another day of cooking and cleaning. I'm sure I don't know how I'll be able to stand all the excitement," Katie said in an appreciably louder voice than she usually used.

Murdoch turned the page and coughed. "Go on you old bat, give it your best shot," he thought, but did not say.

"I guess you'll be doin' your usual exotic social round today, huh?" Katie made Murdoch's 'social rounds' sound positively indecent.

Her husband grunted, shifted position and continued to read.

"Look at the place! This is all we got for all these years."

Murdoch did not look up and was silent.

"There's hardly enough room in this here kitchen to swing a cat." Katie spat out the words.

Murdoch sniffed and gave his attention to *Prince Valiant*. He liked the single-framed cartoon which featured knights and princesses. He found the drawing exquisite, and often wished he could have ridden a richly caparisoned horse as Valiant did. He noted that there was nearly always an elegant castle in the background, usually high on a rocky hill. He wondered how sumptuously furnished were the chambers inside the castle. He imagined hanging tapestries, gold drinking goblets, a giant wolf hound on the carpet in front of a roaring fire and a spitted ox slowly turning.

"Does it have a voice?" He heard Katie ask rhetorically. He knew she was referring to his quietude, so he decided to give her more of it.

"Apparently no!" she continued. "It must have been struck dumb in the night."

Murdoch started to read Ann Landers' response to a man who had written for advice on how to locate his missing wife. He chuckled softly.

"Murdick!" Katie bawled at him.

"Huh?"

"I'm talking to you, b'y."

"Oh yeah?"

"What you doin' today? You taking little Margie for a walk?"

"I imagine I will," he replied, still reading. "I usually do."

"Then I guess you'll be off to play cards at that old Pensioners' Union?"

"I shouldn't wonder," said Murdoch, not taking his eyes from the paper.

"Then back home for supper and watch television?"

"Uh-huh. Sounds about right."

"My God, Murdick, don't you get bored doin' the same old thing day after day?"

"You feelin' alright?" Murdoch asked finally looking up from the sports section and peering at her.

"What the name of time do you mean by that? 'Am I feeling alright'?"

"All morning you been blatherin' and witterin' around like somethin' was sent for and couldn't come. What's up? Is the 'lastic in your drawers too tight? "

Katie glared at him with pure venom, snorted loudly, then stomped away into the front room.

Murdoch stared after her for a second, then returned to his newspaper. "Should never have given them the vote," he muttered under his breath.

Eavesdropping on this marital exchange through the wide-open window, Alex MacDonald sat on the step, stifling his laughter. Katie and Murdoch were always good to put on a show when a fellow was bored, but he knew that as much as they might argue, neither one would have been without the other, come what may.

Across the street a door opened and Margie appeared, accompanied by her mother, Violet. She ushered her daughter across and left her talking to Alex over the battered fence.

"Hi, Alec!"

"Good day, Margie. How's she goin'?"

"Okay, I guess, Alec," said the little girl, "Ma had me to the hospital again yesterday, but they says I'm doin' fine."

"But do you feel okay?"

"Not really. I gets awful weak sometimes, and now and then I has to throw up."

"Well, you take her easy, girl."

"I will, Alec."

"Are you goin' for your walk with Murdick today?"

"Yeah, that's why I come over."

"It's a great day for it. Murdoch's up and about. I heard him a few minutes ago."

Margie walked to the next gate, went to the MacNeils' door and knocked lightly.

Katie opened the door. "Good day. Margie." Over her shoulder she called to her husband. "Murdick! Margie's here!"

"Just let me get me shoes on!" Murdoch shouted back. "Tell her I'll be right there."

"He's on his way, darlin'," said Katie, and disappeared into the house.

Margie wandered over to the fence and kicked at a clump of dandelions. "What you readin', Alec?"

"Oh...it's kind of hard to explain, Margie. It's about a bunch of people in Russia."

"Lemme see."

Alex held the book out.

"*War and Peace.* Looks like it's goin' to take you a while to get through it."

"Yeah, it's kind of long."

"I seen about Russia on the news."

"I guess you must've, but this is about Russia in the olden times. Before I was born."

"Before Murdick was born?"

"Yeah," Alex laughed. "Even before Murdick was born."

"Who's takin' my name in vain?" said Murdoch, appearing in the doorway. "Good day, Margie. Good day, Alec. How's she goin'?"

"Good day, Murdick. You'd best get goin'. Margie's been chompin' at the bit to get her exercise."

"Alright then, let's go, Margie!"

Murdoch took her hand and they edged through the gate and very slowly, almost painfully, moved up the row in the direction of the clifftop.

Violet watched them go then crossed the street. "Good day, Alec."

"Good day, Violet. How's she goin'?"

Violet opened the gate, came in and sat on the steps by Alex's side. She started to sob uncontrollably.

"Hey, Violet." He put his arm around her shoulders. "What's up?"

"It's not so good, Alec. We're going to lose our little angel."

"No!" Alex was aghast. "Who said? What did you find out?"

'They got new bone marrow tests. They told me yesterday when we was at the hospital. They told me she's falling fast."

"Is that definite?"

"Yeah, it's definite. Dr. Khalifa told me he got the report from Halifax."

"Jesus Christ! It don't seem right." Alex shook his head. "Did they tell you how long she's got?"

At that moment Winston Barber drove up and pulled in on the other side of the road.

"Weeks, maybe," said Violet, "Months at most."

"I just don't know what to say, Vi. By Jesus I'm goin' to miss her something wicked. So will old Murdick. And everyone around here."

Violet erupted again in tears and put her head on Alex's shoulder.

At that moment Winston appeared at the gate. "Mr. MacDonald? Alex MacDonald?"

"I'll go now," said Violet, drying her eyes.

"Oh, I'm sorry if I interrupted something," Winston said. "Should I come back some other time?"

"No, that's okay, Mister," said Violet, rising. "I'm on my way. I'll see you, Alec."

"Yeah. Okay, Vi."

Winston held the gate open for her and she re-crossed the road and went into her house.

"I apologize if I've come at a bad time. They told me I might find you here. I'm Winston Barber."

19

After hearing Winston explain the purpose of his visit, Alex agreed to extend all the assistance he needed. He said he was unemployed at the moment and that he could be at Winston's disposal for the next few weeks, if necessary.

As an initial step he suggested they tour the immediate neighborhood on foot so Winston could "get a feel" for the place. During these perambulations, Alex said, he would be happy to answer any questions his new friend might have.

Alex led him up and down the rows of The Hub and of New Aberdeen. These adjoining districts comprised five streets running roughly north-south, intersecting eleven which ran east-west. Almost every plot on these streets was occupied by a house erected by the coal company, and ranged from fifty to eighty years old. Between The Hub and New Aberdeen was a stretch of grass known as the Black Diamond Park, and in the south-west corner of the district was the looming bulk of the dirty, noisy Number 20 colliery.

"How many men work in there, Alex?"

"Alec."

"What?"

"My name is spelt A-l-e-x but we says it as Alec."

"Oh, I see."

"In a while I'm going to take you to see a MacNeil feller. He's name is spelt M-u-r-d-o-c-h, but it's said like Murdick."

"I'll try to bear that in mind, Alec."

"You were askin' 'bout the number of men working here?"

"Yes, I was."

"I don't know for sure, but I'd say 'bout two hundred. There was over six hundred until 'bout twenty years ago."

"That was when the explosion happened?"

"You knows 'bout that? Yeah, seven dead."

"And what is that extraordinary building, Alec?" Winston pointed to a single-story hut surrounded by a stout fence.

"Oh that? That's Stalag Thirteen."

"Stalag Thirteen?"

"That's what we calls it, 'cause of the fence. That's the government liquour store, b'y. The difference between this and the one in *Hogan's Heroes* is that they're always tryin' to break *out* of that one, but they're tryin' to break *into* this one." Alec laughed, then spat some tobacco juice on the side of the road.

"Was this mine operating during the big strike?"

"In 1925? No, that was Number 2, though they used the same shafts."

"Are there many around who can remember that strike?"

"Not a whole lot, but some. I was only a little kid meself then. Murdick, MacNeil is quite a bit older'n me—we'll be seeing him by and by—but you gotta figure that anyone who was an adult then'd have be heading for seventy now."

"Oh, so there would be some who'd remember."

"Oh yeah, but them as were kids at the time, well, their memories'd be a bit rocky."

"Yes, of course."

"We'll see some of them fellers later. There's Danny the Dancer. I'd guess he'd be seventy something."

"Why is he called the Dancer?"

"Dunno. I imagine t'was 'cause he could dance up a storm in his younger days. He's a MacDonald, like me."

"Right."

"Winston, you gotta understand that here in Cape Breton almost everyone's got a nickname. That's so's you can tell one MacDonald from another, or one MacNeil from another—"

"I get you."

"But what you need to know is that the nickname don't necessarily tell you 'bout the guy."

"How do you mean?"

"Well, Dancer's father could've been the original dancer, not him. Take Alec the Bebbler—"

"Alec the what?"

"The Bebbler. He's another MacDonald."

"What does 'bebbler' mean?"

"Nobody's really sure. Some folks calls him Alec the Beveller, but if you asks him, he'll tell you it was because when he was a little feller he's father took him out on the ocean, and he said, 'Ooh daddy, look at the water bebbling around the boat.'"

"Good God."

"Now, take the Horsehit MacKinnons from River Ryan. They been called that for generations because their ancestor kept horses. Then there's the Big Pays."

"The what?"

"The Big Pays. They was called that because in the olden times— well, it ain't all that long ago, actually—when the company docked their pay for rent, church, doctor and groceries at the company store, this feller was left with one cent. That's why him and all who came after him is called the Big Pays."

"That's both funny and sad."

"Yeah. Then there's all kinds of nicknames nobody got a clue 'bout how they got started."

"Tell me some of them."

"Well, lemme see. The Minute Hand. Johnny Biscuit Foot, Tommy Satchel Arse, Lewis Reels, The Carbonears—oh yeah, they was from Newfoundland—the skin-the–doors, The Birds, Lem Ramcat, the Papooses, the Fatterhooks. There's more I'll tell you 'bout if I think on them."

"Amazing." Winston shook his head. "Do you think it would be possible for me to talk to Danny the Dancer? I take it he's…"

"Got his marbles?"

"Yes…still lucid."

"Oh yeah, he's lucid, alright."

"So I'll be able to see him?"

"Likely he'll be in the Pensioners' Union later on. I'll take you down there."

"That's very kind of you, Alex."

"Alec. You're welcome, b'y. But you gotta watch out for the Dancer. You could say Dancer's a bit of a chancer." Alex laughed heartily at his own joke. "What I mean is, he's liable to elaborate—is that the word? No, exaggerate is what I mean. If there was a hundred soldiers with rifles, Dancer would say there was a thousand with cannons."

Alex and Winston walked around the top of the district until they came to the cliff top, where they stood, staring out to sea. The sun was very bright now and picked out every wave and ripple with minute flashes.

"Quite a few of the neighbourhoods in Glace bay is named after collieries, at least by the people who lives there," said Alex. "Most of them pits is closed now. New Aberdeen we just seen; that's always called Number Two by us. Now if you look over there to the south"—he pointed out over the town—"way back there. You see that church? That's Holy Cross and it's in what we calls Caledonia, after the pit. That was Dominion Number 4, which closed about ten years ago."

He turned Winston in an anti-clockwise direction and pointed again. "Further up there is Passchendaele but everybody calls it Number Eleven—"

"After the pit."

"You got the idea, b'y."

"There must have been a lot of mines around here at one time."

"Oh yeah. Over fifty, I guess. Not all at the one time, but over the years."

He turned Winston a bit further until they were facing north. "See them buildings over there by the sea? That's Number Twenty-Six colliery, which was built on the site of the old 1B, and if you looks a bit further up, that's the town of Dominion, where the first mine—Dominion Number One—was sunk in, I think it was in 1890 somethin'."

"It all seems very logical."

They stood motionless, feeling the wind cooling their cheeks. Some gulls wheeled near them. Far out there was a ship inching along the horizon.

Suddenly a cry came drifting on the breeze.

Alex snapped to attention. "Somethin's wrong, b'y. Come on!"

"What is it? Where are we going?"

"Sounds like Murdick is in trouble."

They rushed along the cliff's edge until they saw Murdoch McANeil kneeling in the scrubby grass. Near him was a body.

"Murdick! What's goin' on, b'y?"

"It's Margie. She just collapsed. Help me get her home, will you?"

"Give her to me," said Winston, stepping in. "I'm much bigger than either of you guys."

He gently picked Margie up in his arms, and the sad party slowly made their way towards the houses.

20

Violet had called an ambulance, and Alex and Winston stood by helplessly, waiting for its arrival, watching the little girl now in an apparent coma. Murdoch crouched by her side, holding her hand while her mother quietly sobbed in the doorway.

A siren coming from a south-westerly direction alerted them to an ambulance's imminent arrival.

"That'll be coming down Wallace's Road from St. Joseph's," Alex said.

"I guess," said Violet. "That'd be a lot closer than the General."

"Religion don't matter at a time like this," grunted Murdoch.

They watched as the ambulance came tearing along East Avenue, made a hair-raising turn into the row and screeched to a halt outside the house. Two men jumped out and ran into where Margie was laying.

"Thanks for coming, she—" Violet started to speak, but the attendant cut her off.

"We knows all 'bout Margie, Mrs., don't worry, we'll take it for here."

They carefully placed Margie on a stretcher and slid her in through the rear doors of the vehicle.

"Can I ride with her?" Violet pleaded.

"Sure you can. Hop in the back, Mrs."

"Thank you Mr...." Violet said, turning to Winston.

"Barber. It was nothing, I wish we could have met under better circumstances."

"Yeah, me, too."

She clambered into the ambulance. "Thanks, Murdick. You're a real friend."

"Good luck, Vi."

The three men watched as the van retraced its route along East Avenue, and they walked to the end of the row so they could see it wend its way up Eighth Street, onto Connaught Avenue, and then up the long hill past the cemetery on Wallace's Road.

When it disappeared from sight, Alex turned to Murdoch. "Murdick, this here is Winston. He just arrived a few hours ago. He's in town to see if he can write a movie for Dan Petrie."

"Pleased to meet you, Winston. You got the same name as the feller as won the war."

"He didn't do it single-handed," said Alex.

"I knows that. Anyway, Winston, it's somethin' terrible you had to have this happen on your first day."

"Yes, it is quite upsetting."

"I'd best go report to Katie. Alec, I guess I'll see you fellers at the Pensioners' Union later."

"You bet."

"Look, Mr. Winston, why don't you come have supper with us tonight? I'll tell Katie to kill the fatted calf."

"I'd love to, thank you so much."

"We lives right next to Alec. See yez 'bout six I imagine."

They watched him hobble up the row, then resumed their tour.

They walked along the cliff top and down through Table Head, with the goal of following the shoreline all the way to the wharf at the bottom of Main Street.

"Alex—"

"Alec."

"Sorry, Alec. Murdoch said something strange back there about religion not mattering at a time like this."

"Yeah."

"What did he mean?"

"Thass' a long story, b'y. You sure you wanna hear it?"

"Certainly I do."

"Years back, the miners had money checked off for a hospital and raised money for it with bake sales and all that kind of thing."

"Yes?"

"So finally they built a hospital—the one they took Margie to just now."

"Yes, it's called St. Joseph's, isn't it?"

"It is now, but back then it was called The General."

"But I'm confused. Didn't Violet mention a hospital called the General somewhere else in town?"

"You goin' to let me tell the story, or what?"

"Sorry, go ahead."

"So this General Hospital was what you call ecumenical—no that's the wrong word—non denominational, is what I want. But as time went on the Catholics—I'm one of them, so I ain't carryin' their water here—got a majority on the board and as soon as they did, they passed a motion to bring in the Sisters of St. Joseph to run the place and they changed the name from The General to St. Joseph's."

"That can't have been too popular with the Protestants."

"No, sir. The Protestants was some livid, and they said 'frig this', pulled out, went over to Brookside Street on the other side of town and built their own hospital. And, 'course, they called it the General."

"That's quite a story. But that was in the past. Is there still strong religious feeling today?"

"They says not, but that's bullshit. It's still here. We got two high schools, Morrison and St. Michael's. Why d'you s'pose that is?"

"Religion?"

"Right. And most of the Councillors. In Ward Three you got Angus Blue—you heard of him?"

"No."

"I'll tell you 'bout him later. Well, he's the Catholic and Archie Boyd is the Protestant. In Ward Four, you got Gordon Smith, a Protestant, and Walter MacPhee, a Catholic. It's the same all over."

They went on, past the Marconi monument, strolled along Vivian Street, and down North Street, where Winston had stopped earlier to look at the ocean, and eventually came to the wharf at the junction of Bell and Main streets. They saw a number of fishing boats, some unloading a catch which Winston was unable to identify, and some ill-dressed men gathered behind an old shack.

On closer examination of this group, who were drinking out of a communal bottle, he saw the man who had fallen in front of his car earlier.

"I had a run-in with that guy, a couple of hours ago," Winston said, discreetly pointing him out.

"Lonnie Kelly! Jesus, he's one friggin' pain in the arse. Stay well away from him, b'y."

"I intend to."

"A little while ago we was talking 'bout the 1925 strike. Well, this here harbour was blockaded by the federal government at that time. They sent a warship. I believe it was a frigate. If we sees Dancer later he's liable to say there were four battleships. Anyways, it had its guns trained on the town the whole time."

"Really? Why did they do that?"

"The story goes, they done it to stop supplies comin' to the miners from Russia."

"Russia?"

"Yeah, the feds thought that Comrade Stalin might try to use the strike to stir up trouble."

"Were there Communists here? I mean Canadian Communists?"

"Oh, sure. A feller called J. B. MacLachlan was their leader."

They wandered up Main Street until they came to an enormous red-brown painted building.

"What on earth is that?"

"That's the Miner's Forum, b'y. That's where we has hockey games and the really big meetings."

"Back there you said you'd tell me about this councillor. Blue was it?"

"Oh yeah. Angus Blue. He's quite a character. He's famous because he speaks ignorant and gets himself into shitty mistakes."

"Like what?"

"One time, they had a debate in the council to install some new urinals in the town hall and Angus gets up and says, 'Your Warship, if we're gonna put in new urinals I thinks we should put in some arsenals at the same time'!"

"That's priceless."

"Another time he was in the Legion and they was discussing gettin' a chandelier for the main hall. So Blue says: 'I don't know why we wanna get a chandelier in here 'cos there's not one of us knows how the play the damn thing.'"

"Do you have any more Angus Blue stories?" Winston asked.

"There's all kinds of them, b'y. Just one more, then we'll go to the Pensioners and see who's beating their gums today."

"Alright, go ahead."

"Well, see, Angus is a big Liberal. He's a wheel in the Liberal Party. So one time Lester Pearson comes to town—you heard of him?"

"Maybe, I'm not sure."

"He was the prime minister before this Trudeau feller. Anyways, he come down here for a big meeting and he's after pushing this here bilingualism—"

"French and English?"

"Yeah, that's it. Angus gets up and says he was against it, and says: 'Mr. Chairman, I b'lieve that we should only speak the language of the good Lord hisself, and that's English.' Pearson gets up right after him and says, 'I don't care if you speak English, French or the language of the previous speaker.'"

At length, they passed a large, venerable building called the Firemen's Parlours, then came to Senator's Corner. Across from them was the old house in which the Pensioners' Union members played cards and held their meetings.

"Before we go in," Winston said, "do you know how many Mac-Donalds there are in Cape Breton?"

"I don't know, b'y. Thousands I should think. Pretty near every second person around here is a MacDonald or a MacNeil."

"That's why all the nicknames you were mentioning earlier."

"Yeah. They calls me Bright Alec 'cause I'm always reading. My father was known as Red Tom."

"Because he had red hair?"

"No, b'y, 'cause he was one of them Communists."

They both laughed.

Over in the Melody Café Annie and Gloria were watching them intently. Winston looked up and noticed Annie waving to him, He smiled and waved back.

"You know Annie?"

"Yes, I had a cup of coffee there when I first arrived."

"Oh."

"You certainly have a lot of colourful characters in Glace Bay."

"Do we ever! Here's one of them coming right now."

Alex nodded down the street to where a wiry, one-legged, old man on crutches was propelling himself along at amazing speed. He stopped alongside them, licked his leathery lips and, leaning to one side, spat in the gutter and scratched his groin.

'By the Lord jumpin' Joe Jesus, Alec. How're makin' her, b'y?"

"Good, Billy. How you doin', Billy?"

"Jesus Murphy and Joseph! If I was any better it'd be a mortal sin, b'y. They tells me I looks like hell, but I feels great!"

He spat a long steaming stream of tobacco juice, then peered suspiciously at Winston. "Who in the name of Jesus is this feller? He looks like somethin' was sent for and couldn't come, b'y."

"This here is Winston, Billy."

"How she's goin', Winston?"

"Fine, thank you."

"You ain't from around here, I can tell that."

"No, I'm here to do some research on a possible film."

"I guess it beats workin', b'y," Billy said. "Don't be tellin' me you're goin' over to the Pensioners', Alec?"

"Maybe."

"Don't be wastin' your time with them fellers, b'y. Most of them don't know if our Lord was crucified or killed by the shunt."

"We thought we'd just call in and see who's there."

"It's your funeral, b'y," said Billy and continued on his way round the corner.

21

Annie Pyke was thirty-two years old, from a good family, none of whose members had been in trouble with the law, and lived in a well-kept, presentable house. And she was the proprietor of the Melody Café, a popular venue which produced a steady profit, most of which she had managed to save against "a rainy day." She had kept this from her father and her fiancé, partly to forestall them from making demands on her capital for frivolous purposes, and partly because she did not regard it as any of their business.

She knew she was smart, able and attractive and was widely considered respectable. Annie's late mother, Euphemia, had been the daughter of a small Sydney merchant and had inherited his pretensions, if not his money, which had gone to her brothers. Respectability was something she valued highly in others, and craved for herself and her own family. Unfortunately, but not tragically, she never attained it because Arthur was a coal miner by occupation, and a rough diamond, if not a coarser mineral, by nature.

Since she could not appreciably raise herself above the other mining families amongst whom she dwelt, she was determined that her daughter should succeed where she had failed. She taught Annie to dress well, to carry herself upright and not slouch, and to try, in so far as was possible, to associate with a "better kind of people" than themselves.

Annie had not disappointed her in these respects, but in two others she had, in Mrs. Pyke's opinion, ignominiously failed. The first was that her manner of speech remained very much similar that of the rest of the community, slurring her words, misusing grammar, and employing colloquialisms. The second area in which Annie had proved a severe disappointment to Euphemia was that she had made the same mistake her mother had made; she had gotten mixed up with Donnie MacNeil, another miner.

She had met Donnie at a dance at the Row Street Athletic Club in Bridgeport, the farthest flung of Glace Bay's districts.

They had chatted as best they could above the hullabaloo, and danced a little. She did not like it there because it was too noisy, too crowded, and because her mother would think most of those enjoying themselves as the "wrong kind" of people.

As she was pushing her way out, Donnie asked her for a date and, as much to get rid of him as anything else, she agreed.

Thus began a relationship which grew into a habit which they both continued because neither had an obvious alternative lover, and neither had the heart to break it off. Eventually they settled into a comfortable, unexciting, state, meeting at predictable times, going to predictable places and doing predictable things.

And when Donnie proposed, with the ring Annie had chosen and paid for, it seemed a logical extension of their association. On that occasion, they decided that they would be married at such time as they could afford to buy a house, but they never mentioned the subject again.

Involuntarily shaking her head, Annie thought of the sporadic occasions on which they had furtive sexual encounters in various motels in the area. Donnie always went to the desk and booked the room, while she loitered on the street a few blocks away. When he had acquired the room key he would drive back, pick her up, and drive her, crouched down in the back seat, to their unit. It was an ungainly, grubby, disreputable business and, when she considered the indignity, the creases in her clothing and Donnie's frequently inexpert performances, she wondered if it was worth the trouble.

"I'm just nippin' out," said Annie, taking off her apron.

"Where you goin'" asked Marlene.

"Got a bit of business to do."

"Right," Gloria said

"I won't be long," said Annie, opening the café door.

In various romance novels, Annie had read that sex could be intense, passionate and exciting. Participants were said to see stars, hear bells ringing and experience Vesuvius-like climaxes, but so far her limited amorous adventures in Glace Bay had produced none of those sensations. But as she looked across the street to where the men were talking, she just *knew* all of those senses—and more—would be achieved with Winston Barber. This made her more than ever resolved to contrive the circumstances which would culminate in this consummation.

"You know where she's goin', don't ya?" Gloria said to her co-worker.

"No. Where's she goin'?"

"Across the street to see if that New York feller is still hanging around."

"You think?"

"I know so. Tell ya somthin' else too, Marlene."

"What's that, Gloria?"

"I bet I gets his ass before she does."

"Ooh!" Marlene gave her a shocked look. "You wouldn't!"

"Wouldn't I just."

"But he's as old as your father."

"I don't give a rat's ass how old he is. Just watch me!"

Across the street, Winston and Alex were about to go over to the Pensioners' Union when Annie, pretending to turn into Carol's drug store, 'accidentally' brushed up against Winston. She felt something like a cross between an electric shock and a rush of hot water.

"Oh, it's you. I am sorry. I was in a bit of a rush. I didn't see you," she lied, stammering.

"Oh. Hi, Annie. No problem. Nothing serious, I hope."

"What?"

"The drug store. I hope you're not sick."

"Oh no." She regained her composure. "Say, I just thought of somethin'. D'you want to go to the John Allen Cameron concert?"

"Who's he?"

"Oh he's great," Alex intervened. "He sings Scottish and Cape Breton music."

"Where's the concert taking place?"

"Right there," Annie said, pointing up Union Street to the Savoy Theatre.

"Oh. Okay, why not? Where would I get tickets?"

"Leave that to me," said Annie. "I'll get them and let you know."

"Thanks, Annie. Now, Alec, we'd better get over to the Pensioners'' Union."

As Annie walked back to the café, outwardly she was smiling serenely, but inwardly a small hurricane was taking place, and her heart was pounding nineteen to the dozen.

"That was quick," said Gloria.

"Yeah."

"Did you see that New York feller?"

"What if I did?"

"You don't wanna be two-timin' your Donnie."

"You shut your mouth and get on with your work," Annie said hotly. "Go scrub that sink again. It's right filthy."

22

A DEVCO truck stopped to let Alex and Winston cross the road. They waited until other traffic had also halted before leaving the sidewalk.

"Come on, Alex, b'y!" the truck driver shouted. "What in the Jesus you waitin' for, a royal salute or somethin'?"

"Like you're in a rush to go anywhere, Reggie," Alex called back. "It's not like you do any work, sittin' up there like an oriental potentate."

"Whatever the hell that is, you can shove it up your arse."

"See you, Reggie."

"Not if I see you first."

They pushed open the door of the Pensioners' Union to reveal about thirty men crammed into three adjoining rooms of the ground floor of an old house set back from Main Street. The place was extremely hot, and the air was thick with tobacco smoke, sweat and the singular smell which is often associated with old men.

Some of the men were standing in a corner, apparently arguing an arcane detail of union history. All them, varying in age from 50 to 90, had been members of District 26 of the United Mine Workers of America, which had been established in Cape Breton sixty years previously. Since then the area had seen a tumultuous and violent history, the men frequently battling the coal company and not uncommonly fighting among themselves, all of which provided a rich catalogue of colourful events to be thrashed out again and again wherever miners and former miners gathered.

Those who were not holding forth in the corner were sitting at various tables, playing cards.

Seeing them enter, Murdoch put down his cards and rose to meet them. "There you are, Alec. Come on in, Winston, and meet the gang."

He banged on a table for silence. "Just so's you know, this here is Winston Barber, who's come from away to write a movie for our own Dan Petrie. I hope yez'll make him welcome." He nodded towards Alex. "I'm guessing you knows this other feller."

"Do we ever," called one man at the back. "How the Jesus did us ever allow him through the door?"

"Bring your books with you, Alec?" yelled another man.

Murdoch conducted them around the premises, introducing Winston to various characters. As he did so, they were heckled from other tables, setting off a raft of good-natured banter.

"Winston, I'd like you to meet Billy Pitman."

"How's she goin', b'y?"

"You're wasting your time, Billy, they ain't goin' to put your ugly mug in no movie."

"It's a damn sight better'n yours," retorted Billy. "You'd break the friggin' camera!"

"And this is Archie MacIntyre. We calls him Archie the Buck."

"Good day, Winston," Archie said. He was a short, plump, pink man with a big smile and a shiny bald head. "My crowd came here because they wired the old country to send more brogues, but they didn't hear it right and sent more rogues."

"And the rest of us been payin' the price ever since!" hooted a man by the window.

"This here is Russell MacPhee."

"How you're making her, b'y?" Russell asked.

"Russell's already got his bags packed for Hollywood," cried Billy.

"Yes sir," said Russell. "This is my big break. I always knew I had talent."

"Yeah. Talent for bullshit!" interjected Archie.

"Shut up, b'ys. I'm tryin' to introduce Winston to you gang of thieves and I can't hear meself think," Murdoch said, getting riled. "Now here's another Murdick, b'y, Murdick Matheson."

"How do, Wilson," said Matheson, a tall, rangy man with no teeth and two fingers missing from one hand.

"Winston. I'm fine, Mr. Matheson."

"And over here we got Joe Nearing," said Murdoch.

"I knows what you're looking for, Joe," yelled Billy. "You're anglin' to get to meet that Raquel Welch."

"Yeah, and I could still show her a thing or two."

"She'd run a mile before you had the chance, b'y!"

"They're all jealous of me, Winston," said Joe. "They can't stand my attraction for the women."

The trio finally worked their way to a corner table near the back door, where Arthur Pyke was sitting with a tall, heavy-set man with a craggy face, fleshy lips and a large nose. His hair was streaked across his scalp and he wore loose-fitting khaki clothes, which might have been army surplus. He wore a Canadian Legion tie and had a flower in his buttonhole. It was clear that in an ideal world this man should have been an actor, as he was talking loudly to Arthur, accompanied by wild arm and hand gestures.

"Excuse us gents," said Murdoch. "Winston, this here is the famous Danny the Dancer. Danny, this is Winston Barber. He's here to write a script for a movie. He's looking for accounts of the olden days."

Obviously an old ham, Dancer rose and grandiloquently welcomed them to his table. There was little question that he was a man who constantly played to the crowd, no matter where he happened to be.

He addressed Winston in a deep, stentorian, sonorous voice. "Welcome, my young friend. Please be seated. Rest assured you have come to the right place."

Winston sat down and outlined to Dancer his tentative plan to centre his screenplay on the 1925 strike. From time to time Murdoch and Arthur inserted a few comments, but Dancer held the floor for most of their interview.

"I was just a youngster at the time," said Murdoch, "but already by then I'd been in the pit for ten years or so."

"I'm older than you, Murdick," said Dancer. "I remember you when you was a trapper."

"That's right, I was. Started when I was eleven."

"What's a trapper?" Winston asked.

"The company had young boys operating the flaps between the levels," Arthur explained.

"The traps were like doors," said Dancer, seeing that Winston did not understand. "The boys had to open and shut them to let the men and the ponies through—"

"Ponies?"

"Yes, b'y, they had scores of these little horses to pull the wagons of coal. The trappers pulled the flaps back to let the animals go through, then closed them again afterwards."

"Why couldn't they just stay open?"

"They were needed to control the circulation of the air throughout the mine."

"How old were you in 1925, Dancer?" Arthur asked.

"A few days after thirty, and what a strapping young laddy buck I was, I can tell you. After I did my apprenticeship as a trapper, I was loading coal with my old man. That was in Caledonia mine. Later we transferred to Number Two. We was there at the time of the big strike."

"Tell me about that."

"The company posted a wage reduction of thirty percent," Murdoch said.

"Imagine!" Dancer's voice became histrionic. "A *reduction* when we was already near starvation! Were we going to stand for that? No, sir! We were not!"

"We come out," said Murdoch. "Hundred percent, wasn't it?"

"One hundred percent!" Dancer affirmed.

"What does that mean?"

"It means no pumps, no fans. Other times we'd leave them continue to operate so the mine wouldn't get flooded."

"Would that be seawater?" Winston asked.

"Some, but mostly groundwater. It came through the slate, so it was so acidic it corroded metal," Dancer said. "Then the company retaliated by sending in the troops."

"They called them 'provincial police'," Arthur said.

"Scum!" shouted Dancer, now on his feet. "Scum and criminals recruited off the Halifax waterfront. Most of those curs couldn't even sit upright in the saddle."

"Boy, my father was after cursing them fellows something wicked," Murdoch said.

"And never were curses more richly deserved!"

The whole room was now giving its attention to Dancer. In response to his audience, he started to pace up and down, flapping his arms. "The Lord himself had forsaken such vermin. They came for us loaded for bear."

The crowd had heard all this before, some of them many times, but they never tired of the entertainment. Dancer was now in a state of high dudgeon, with sweat running down his bright red face. He whirled around, his eyes blazing, his arms flailing.

"We faced the forces of the Devil himself. We stood shoulder to shoulder and looked down the rifle muzzles into the eyes of the denizens of hell."

Dancer sat down, gasping for breath. Someone pushed a mug of tea in front of him, which he gulped down.

"How did it all end, Dancer?" Winston asked.

"We were beat." Dancer slouched back in his chair, exhausted from his exertions. "They appointed a Royal Commission. In the end we still had to take a reduction and they closed several of the mines."

Winston thanked Dancer and, waving and nodding to the room, he and Alex took their leave.

Archie McIntyre came out with them. "Bet you never heard the like of that before, Winston," he said.

"No, it was like a Shakespearean play."

"The way he was a-huffin' and a-puffin' it looked more like Custer's last stand," said Archie, grinning.

23

When Donnie MacNeil came off shift that afternoon, he went straight home instead of calling in at the Melody Café to talk to Annie. Donnie called it "checking in" as if it were both a legal and a moral obligation, and he felt uncomfortable complying because he was ill at ease in his work clothes in the café, and he resented being what one of his work mates had unkindly called "Annie's little dog."

He was well aware that he would be punished for today's lapse by Annie's sulking, certainly for hours and perhaps for days, but he didn't need talk today. He needed to get his boots off, stretch out and have a Tenpenny, or maybe three.

It was not that he did not like Annie—he told himself he loved her—but their routine was tiring and its sameness was starting to be boring. He imagined that if they were married and had their own place, Annie would be more relaxed. She would only have to "put on the dog" when they went out, something they would not have to do as much as they were required to do at present.

He thought that reaching these conclusions might enable him to reach another. He weighed the benefits of their liaison against the disadvantages. Put in its crudest form, he decided, it was a piece of tail twice a week against the stress, the bother and the nagging.

On that premise, he determined that their relationship could not continue in its present form, and if it did not change, it would have to end.

However, on the other hand, when he anticipated that in any event he would get married someday, and that there would also be drawbacks and downsides to that partnership, he was forced to conclude that any hard and fast decisions should be postponed. He would wait until fate intervened and made the decision for him.

In this unsettled state of mind, he went into the house, kicked off his boots, threw his jacket on the banister and dropped his lunch can on the floor. The can was, as always, empty. That was because, on his way home, Donnie had given the banana bread to the MacLellans' dog. He despised banana bread, and whenever it appeared in the can, the dog received a treat.

One thing was certain: His mother must never know he disliked anything she baked, and certainly not that her comestibles had been fed to a canine.

"You home, Ma?" he called out.

"In the kitchen, b'y."

Katie was sitting at the table, her tiny spectacles on the end of her nose, holding Dorothy's letter, which by now showed signs of having been handled and re-read many times.

"There you are, Ma."

"'Course I am. Where the hell should I be?"

"Where's the old man?"

"Down the Pensioners'. Where else?"

Donnie walked over to the stove, poured himself a cup of the black tea which had been steeping for hours, took one sip, grimaced and put the cup down. Then he went to the fridge and extracted a bottle of Tenpenny. removed the cap and took a long swig.

"Ahh!" He wiped his mouth on his sleeve. "Anything new?"

"Little Margie collapsed when she was out walking with your father. An amb'lance came and took her to the hospital."

"Jesus, that's too bad."

"Watch your mouth! Don't be blasphemin'. That child may not

be coming out, is my guess."

"The poor, little mite." said Donnie, after draining the bottle. "What's that you got there?"

"A letter from our Dorothy. They're getting a new house, her and Tom. She says they want me and Murdick to go live with them."

"In Toronto?!"

"Yes, in Toronto. That's where they live."

"Huh!" said Donnie, the embryo of a thought forming itself in his mind. "Toronto. Hmm."

"That all you got to say?"

"Would you like that, Ma?"

"Yes, I would, Donnie, b'y! I've lived here for fifty some years."

"Well, a change would sure do you good." The embryo was beginning to form a blastocyst.

"Yes indeed it would."

"Not to mention being near them grandkids." The blastocyst had become a fetus. "And our Phemie, Wayne, and Theresa are up in them parts, too."

"I don't see nearly enough of them, Donnie. My four eldest had to move away to find work when they was quite young." Katie nodded, then as an afterthought added, "'Course I'd miss you and Rita."

"Yeah. We'd miss you too, Ma," said Donnie. A fully-formed idea had been born. "But we could come up to see yez from time to time. And you could always visit back home."

He got another beer from the fridge and poured his mother a cup of the dark and bitter brew. Yes, he thought, I left it to fate and now fate has intervened and provided me with a solution.

He pondered whether he should give voice to the idea, or let someone else suggest it. He decided to risk it. If he got his mother onside at the outset, the chances were that she would adopt it as her own idea.

He plunged in. "When I think on it, Ma, it could be the answer to a lot of problems."

"Oh yeah?" Katie gave him a quizzical look.

"Me and Annie could finally get married…" He left the statement hanging for a few seconds, then tentatively added, "Maybe we could live here."

"Ah." Katie smiled tolerantly. "You got all the bases covered, haven't you?"

Embarrassed, Donnie turned away to look through the window.

"No, but you're right. It'd be the perfect solution. Listen, Donnie, I'll make a deal with you. You help me talk Murdick into it, and I'll see to it the place is yours."

"Alright, Ma. It's a deal!" said Donnie, grinning widely. "But I'm guessin' it won't be easy."

"You said a mouthful there, b'y. Your da will be kickin' and screamin', I'll bet."

"That's for sure."

Donnie looked around and noticed a stack of crockery on the counter. "Why're the special plates put out? We only sees them when you wants to show off to someone."

"Don't be gettin' saucy with me, b'y. Otherwise I could change me mind about the house."

"Sorry, Ma. I was only sayin'. I didn't mean nothin' by it."

"Hmm. If you must know, we got a guest for supper."

"Who? Who's comin'?"

"You sound like an old owl, b'y. Your father got himself a new friend. He's that feller that's come from New York to see about a movie they're gonna make here. Winston is his name."

"Ah, Jesus. That means I gotta put on a clean shirt, don't it?"

"Indeed it does! Now listen to me, b'y. You be on your best behaviour or you could blow your chances of ever getting' this house."

"Yeah. Alright, Ma."

Donnie had a strange feeling that he had not jumped from the frying pan into the fire, but rather that he had carried the pan with him into the flames.

But it might all be worth it, he thought. If he could pull it off, Annie would be some pleased. It might even get him extra tail, and that would be a bonus to the main prize.

24

"Don't get me wrong, Winston," said Archie MacIntyre. "I makes fun of Dancer 'cause he always showin' off, but he's right about them times, alright. They was mighty tough."

They were still standing outside the pensioners' union. Indicating a bench by the front door, Archie sat down and bade Alex and Winston join him.

Archie rolled himself a cigarette and lit it, blowing smoke rings into the air. They soaked up the strong sunshine for several minutes before Murdoch came out and stood by them.

"Room for a little one?" he asked. "Budge up."

They did their best to make space for him on the bench. Several passers-by smiled as they went down the street.

"Look at that," said a man on a bicycle. "A rose and three thorns."

"Don't give them any money, Mister," said a woman pushing a baby carriage. "They'll only drink it."

"I shouldn't wonder if that bench don't give way under the weight," A taxi driver said to his fare. "I figure there must be a thousand pounds there between them."

"Don't be so foolish, Joe," Archie retorted. "Every one of us is light as a feather."

"I've heard that there was a harsh man in charge of the mines in 1925," Winston said. "Is that so, Archie?"

"You got that right, Winston. The boss of the company was a feller called Roy Wolvin. From Montreal, I think he was."

"The evilest man who ever hung a pair of balls over a piss pot," Murdoch said with venom. "The spawn of Satan, he was."

"You know what he said when we come out on strike?" Archie asked Winston.

"No, what?"

"'Let them stay out three weeks or three months, it matters not. They can't stand the gaff'!"

"Can't stand the gaff!" Murdoch and Alex echoed with great feeling.

"What does that mean?" Winston asked.

"The sufferin' and privation. The starvation."

"Oh, I see. And were there many who did starve?"

"Well," Archie looking knowingly at Murdoch. "It's kind of hard to say. I know some of us, like Dancer, say that they did, but it not somethin' you could prove."

"For sure many went hungry," Alex said.

"Oh yes, many went hungry. I think it's safe to say that many were brought to the brink of starvation," Murdoch said.

"That's when another famous saying came into Cape Breton history, b'y. 'Carryin' the bag,'" said Archie. "That meant roamin' the countryside, scrounging potatoes or stealing the odd chicken, in order to feed the kids."

"I was sent out to carry the bag, Archie."

"Indeed you was, Murdick. Sometimes we got a coupla apples and, if we was lucky, maybe a rabbit."

"I heard tell that the Quaker Oats company sent railcars full of oats down here. Is that true?" Alex interjected.

"Yes, sir. I remembers seein' them in a siding up yonder. And I b'lieve we got a thousand dollars from Russia!"

"From Russia?"

"From the coal miners of the Union of Soviet Socialist Republics!"

"That must have been controversial."

"Holy moly! Was it ever! The bishops and priests was up in arms about it."

"I imagine they would be," said Winston, "So, did you stand the gaff?"

"That we did, b'y, said Archie. "We stood the friggin' gaff for five months of misery and despair."

As the men sat discussing the strike, Gloria Maddin clocked off her shift for the day and stepped out of the Melody Café into the bright sunshine. She looked about her to see if any potential admirers were in evidence. Seeing Winston across the street, she hitched up her already short skirt and pulled back her shoulders, because she had read that it enhanced her ample bosom.

"So, I guess the men didn't win the strike."

"No, like Dancer said in there earlier," Archie said, "it was a total disaster. Lower wages and fewer jobs."

"Hi, Alec!" Gloria had ostentatiously sashayed over the road and now stood a few feet away. "Hello, Mr. MacNeil. How are you, Mr. Macintyre?"

The older men eyed her, each guarding their own thoughts, memories and regrets. They were pondering what-ifs and maybes.

Archie recalled a girl he had met over fifty years ago who had looked very like this one. She could have been *the* one, but her father didn't like him because he was too "buckish". It was just as well, he reflected, because his Katie had turned up trumps, and had seen him through good and hard times.

Murdoch saw in Gloria a woman called Muriel from whom he had a narrow escape when he was twenty. *His* Katie had stepped in and saved the day, although it had not come without a price.

Winston did not have to wonder. He had known dozens like Gloria and he knew she was his for the asking, and he knew it would happen entirely on his terms, wherever and whenever he wanted. He was not an inconsiderate or unkind man, but he had a wealth of experience and a deep understanding of human nature.

"Hello, there," Gloria said archly to Winston. "How are you?"

"Fine, thank you. Don't you work in the café? You were—"

"Cleaning the windows? Yes. Are you havin' yourself a good day?"

"Fine, thanks. Alec here is giving me the guided tour."

"So where you taking him tonight, Alec? The tavern, I shouldn't wonder."

"No, he's comin' to my house for supper," Murdoch interposed.

"Huhuh. Well, have a nice time. See you around. Soon, maybe."

"Yup. I hope so. Bye bye."

Her heels click-clacked up the street and could be heard after she had disappeared from view.

Archie took a last puff of his cigarette, stubbed it out on the ground and rubbed his chin. "What d'you think, Murdick? I got a feeling Winston here is gonna be quite the hit with the girls."

"Shouldn't wonder if he'll be putting his shoes under that one's bed," Murdoch said, nodding in the direction of Gloria's exit.

"Yeah, coupla days and likely you'll be bedding half the women in town, Winston."

"Somehow I doubt that," Winston said.

"Save some for me, Winston," said Alec. "I haven't been laid since Christ was in kindergarten. These old fellers are past it, but I ain't."

"Watch your mouth, sonny," Archie growled. "there's many a good tune played on an old fiddle, b'y."

"But you'd have to get some new strings put on first," Murdoch said, nudging Archie in the ribs. "Remember the Macintyre clan motto, *Per Ardua*. Through adversity."

"Yeah, yeah. While I'm getting re-stringed, I can hear you now, Murdick, going with that girl, singing the MacNeil clan motto. *Buaidh no bas!*"

"What does that mean?" Winston asked.

"Conquer or die," said Archie, almost collapsing with laughter.

25

When The Dominion Coal Company built the McNeils' house after the end of the Great War in 1919, it comprised two rooms upstairs and two down. Those on the ground floor were an average-sized kitchen and a large living area. The company did not consider the working classes either worthy or desirous of having anything as fancy as a 'dining room' or a bathroom. It was not considered likely that a miner's family would need to entertain by having dinner parties and the like, and if anyone needed to attend to calls of nature, there was what was known as a 'one holer' in a shed in the backyard.

The performance of ablutions, it was assumed, would be conducted in a large tin tub on the kitchen floor, with hot water provided from a large kettle on the coal-fired hob. In the early days, the men would take their baths after coming home from work, and the women would take theirs when the men were at work. Later, washhouses were installed at the pits and the men cleaned themselves on the premises after their shifts ended.

These were occasions for the exchange of male gossip, information, ribaldry and insults. It was not uncommon for men to scrub each other's backs, or to sing hymns and popular songs. But if, whether by accident or mean intent, one of the men commented inappropriately on a woman from another miner's family, sparks could fly and men would come to blows.

Since Murdoch had been able to buy the house in 1945, with the help of the Coady Credit Union, he had made a number of alterations as deemed necessary and as finances could afford.

One project at a time, he had installed upstairs a tiny but adequate bathroom by severely reducing the size of the main bedroom, and erected a partition in the other room to create two very small sleeping quarters. In the early years, very small children slept with their parents, but were segregated when they grew older.

Downstairs, over Katie's objections, he had slightly reduced the size of both kitchen and living room to create a third, cramped, area which was reserved for dining at Christmas, Easter and the infrequent visits by the extended family. This room had lace curtains, cream wallpaper, and dark, shiny furniture which had been purchased because it looked much more expensive than it actually was.

In the one dresser which the room could accommodate were kept the 'good' china, the 'sliver' cutlery, snow-white tablecloth and napkins, and the cruet in the form of two tiny, brightly coloured Toby jugs. Also, it was here, hidden under layers of tissue paper, that Katie kept her 'treasures', which included letters from a sister long gone; ivory candles; a few horse brasses; shiny, striped pebbles taken from a beach when she was a girl; and faded photographs of her parents.

It was in the 'special' room that Winston found himself that evening, squeezed around the table laid with the second-best tablecloth, a somewhat abraded, pale yellow linen covering. While he, Donnie and Murdoch were chatting and laughing over reminiscences of their visit to the Pensioners' Union, Katie scuttled round them, putting out dishes of pickles, a plate of sliced bread, a dish of butter and drinking glasses.

"Did you ever have salt cod and pork scraps before, Winston?" Murdoch asked.

"I can't say I have. It sounds…er…interesting. What is it exactly?"

"The finest kind of food you can get," pronounced Donnie with assurance.

"You soaks the cod in water overnight, then you boils it up—"

"You do NOT boil it!" Katie remonstrated. "You simmers in gently for a few minutes, that's all. Easy to see that there's one feller around here who never does any cookin'. And that's Murdick. What d'you think of that, Winston? Been married half a century and I don't b'lieve he's so much as boiled an egg in all that time."

"G'way with you, woman. I cooked them times you was sick. And the times when the kids come."

"By the jumpin's! He got no memory neither! You put the kettle on the stove, is all. The rest was done by Dorothy, Rita or me sisters."

"*Leigh e air*, woman! I'm tryin' to tell the man. Don't be listenin' to her, Winston. Now, where was I?"

"Tellin' him about the supper," Donnie prompted.

"Oh yeah. Well, you had the salt cod with boiled spuds, masses of fried onions and scrunchions—that's what we calls the pork scraps. It's some good, I can tell you."

"Unless the scrunchions is too soft or too hard," said Donnie.

"It's a real art, that is," said Katie, plonking down a huge bowl of potatoes. "It takes years of practice to get it right. The trick is you got to stand over them, testin' every now and then to make sure they're crunchy, but only just. If you cooks them any more they'll break your teeth."

"Yeah, that's happened to me more than once," Murdoch said.

"Me too," said Donnie, "but gettin' them too soft is worse. They're right chewy and squidgy."

"There you are!" Katie said, putting steaming dishes of food in front of them. "Let's see how you get on with that lot!"

After the salt cod and pork scraps—which was a pleasant revelation to Winston-- Katie served a huge apple pie, which they had with ice cream. Winston could not recall when he had eaten so much at a single sitting, and he was greatly relieved when Murdoch announced that they were moving into the living room.

There, they sprawled out in armchairs bought from Woolco in Sydney River, and Katie offered them tea or coffee. Murdoch went to a sideboard and returned with two bottles of rum: Governor General, which was a golden colour, and Lamb's Navy, which was almost black.

"Will you have a snort, Winston?"

"Just a drop, please."

"Do you want some of the good stuff"—he held up the Lamb's—"or this no-seeum's piss?"

"Language!" Katie shouted from the kitchen.

"I'll take the piss, Dad," said Donnie.

"Donnie!" Katie bawled.

"I guess I'll have the black stuff," said Winston.

While Murdoch was pouring the rum, Katie came in, a cup of tea in hand, and perched in a rocking chair near the window. This was *her* chair, where she could gently rock, listen to conversation in the room and spy on the neighbours at the same time.

"It's getting late," said Winston. "I should be thinking about getting back to Sydney."

"Where you stayin' Winston?" Donnie asked.

"At the Isle Royale Hotel."

"Jesus, that's right fancy, that place."

"Wait a while," Katie said. "Our Rita should be back in a minute. You have to meet her."

"Rita's your other child?"

"I should say so," said Katie somewhat indignantly. "I got three and one dead. One of them's away in Ontario. Just Rita and the baby here now."

"You're the baby, hey, Donnie?"

"Some baby!" Murdoch exclaimed. "Did you see the way he ate?"

There was a noise of keys jingling at the front door.

"That'll be Rita now," Murdoch said. "Do you fancy another shot of rum, Winston?"

"Oh, no thanks. I have to drive."

The door was sticking so it did not open immediately. Donnie jumped up, went over and gave it a shove.

"This is Rita," he said.

"My oldest girl," said Katie.

Rita, startled by Winston's unexpected presence, stood motionless.

"C'mon, girl, put the board in the hole!" Murdoch cried.

"I'm Winston," he said, rising, going towards her, and taking her hand. "I'm pleased to meet you."

"Likewise, I'm sure," she said, staring and not letting go of his hand. Something like an electric current was running from his hand, through hers and up her arm, tingling and warming her insides, making it difficult to break the connection.

Oh my God, she thought, but did not say, this man is some kind of miracle which has landed here. Those eyes! They were like wells of deep, luxurious sensuality.

As dozens of thoughts and feelings contended within her, she came to conclusions which she thought, but did not say, were realistic, practical and just, just, conceivably possible. She knew this man was not for love, for life, for marriage, or even for a meaningful relationship, although never having had one, she was unsure about that. But she was sure he was for a one-time, blessed, celebratory, ceremonious, phantasmagorical encounter.

"How you doin', Winston?"

"Fine. Your mother has crammed me so full of good food I can hardly move."

"That sounds like Ma, alright," she said. He is so well spoken too,

and polite, not like Donnie and other lads around here, she thought
It is so nice to come across manners.

Finally, she managed to let his hand drop.

"I must go now. Thanks everyone for a great evening. Katie, an absolutely fabulous supper. Just wonderful."

He is just wonderful, Rita thought, but did not say.

"You're quite welcome. Come again, Winston," Katie said.

"You'll be up again to Bright Alec's, so I'll see you soon," said Murdoch, raising his glass of rum.

Go on girl, Rita told herself, go ahead and make your move. If you have the courage.

"I still got my coat on, so I'll see you to your car," she said, exultant to discover that she *did* have the courage.

Donnie smirked and Murdoch and Katie exchanged surprised glances as Winston and Rita left.

26

It was on one of those very rare summer evenings when an event usually reserved for the fall occurred. When Rita and Winston came out into the row, both the sun and moon could be seen in the sky.

For a few moments they turned in a circle, marvelling at the phenomenon revealed before their eyes. It would only exist for a short time because it was already darkening, and rolling, black clouds drifted across the lunar half of the firmament.

"Wow!" Rita cried. "Did you ever see the like of that, Winston?"

"Once or twice. I think it was when I was in Italy."

"You've been to Italy? Oh, I'd love to go there. I ain't been out of Nova Scotia."

"Really?"

"Yeah, I've only been to the mainland a coupla times when I went with *Granaidh* on the train to Halifax."

"For a treat, was it?"

"No way, it was for some kind of medical treatment for Granny?"

"Oh."

"That was some adventure. I was only a teenager at the time."

"Is your grandmother still alive?"

"No, she's been dead some time. She was ninety-eight when she went."

They hitched themselves up and sat on the car's hood. The few flickering street lights came on and weakly created pale pools of light on the ground. From a nearby house a record player was bringing Jim Reeves' *I love You Because You're You* to them on the slight breeze.

Across the street, Violet's house was in total darkness. From several streets away a dog barked. At some distance, unseen by Winston and Rita, a female figure lurked in the gathering darkness.

"Where you stayin' Sidney, Winston?"

"As I told your parents, the Isle Royale."

"I've never been inside there. What's it like?"

"Okay. Much like every other hotel."

"I wouldn't know. I was never in a hotel. The times I went to Halifax with *Granaidh* we stayed at a boarding house. I remember it was called Winnie's Lodge. Weird, I should remember that, don't you think?"

"Not especially."

"I know you gotta go," she said, sliding off the car, "It was lovely to meet you, Winston."

"It was lovely to meet you, too," said Winston, leaning down and giving her a small, gentle kiss on the cheek.

Rita softly savoured the kiss for a split second, then recoiled, wondering what snooping neighbours might think.

"I hope I see you again," she said, flustered, yet entranced.

"Me too," Patrick said as he climbed into his car.

Cow-eyed, she watched him go, then turned back into the house, thinking her parents would want to know what kept her for so long. Thus it was that Rita did not see that at the end of the street, before it turned into the road out of town, Winston's headlights illuminated a woman standing on the sidewalk, frantically waving him down.

He pulled up, thinking the woman was in distress and was about to get out when she marched up to the car, opened the passenger door and got in.

It was Gloria. *Gloria in excelsis*, who was even more scantily clad than usual and had clearly gone to the limits with her hair and makeup.

"Hi there, handsome," she said, smiling like a door-to-door salesman. "I said to myself, I think thass Winston's car, and sure enough it was."

"Hello again. You're...?" Winston knew her name well enough as he had committed it to memory, but experience had taught him it was not wise to appear at all eager.

"Gloria."

"Gloria, right. What're you doing on the streets alone at this time of night? Just happened to be in the neighbourhood, did you?"

"This is not New York, y'know. It's quite safe around here."

"So, were you visiting friends?"

"Thass right. I was visitin' friends," she lied.

"You look like you just came from a party, or a dance."

"I likes to look me best," she added archly: "You never knows who you're gonna run into."

"Indeed, you don't."

"You ain't heading my way by any chance, are you?"

"I could be," Winston said coolly, playing the game.

It was a familiar game, one he had played many times. An age-old game, in which the culmination was known, but in which tradition determined that certain steps had to be followed. Rather like Lovat's model for experiencing a religious event, it was a structured ritual, involving the stages of preparation, climax, celebration, and return.

As long as the prescribed steps in this game were observed, it allowed the participants to tell themselves that, whatever transpired, they were not being promiscuous.

"Thass great, b'y. I'll tell you where to go."

"I'm sure you will."

She guided him through town to a street where there were a number of large, older houses, former residences of company officials, which were now in a poor state of repair. She told him where to park up, then wriggled in the seat to ride her skirt higher.

"I guess you'll be comin' up, won't you," she said confidently.

"I guess I could."

They climbed up an outside wooden staircase to the third floor, where Gloria had a tiny apartment comprising a bed-sitting room, a minuscule bathroom, and a recess containing a small stove and a miniature fridge.

"Sit yourself down, Winston," she said.

Since there was nowhere to sit other than the bed, Winston plonked down, grabbed some pillows, and propped himself up.

Gloria momentarily disappeared into the bathroom, and when she came out she started rummaging in a cupboard. She withdrew a bottle from inside and waved it about.

"Y'know what this is, Winston?"

"No, I don't."

"This here is lemon gin. D'you know what we calls it in Cape Breton?"

"Why don't you tell me?"

"We calls it pant remover." She cackled with laughter.

"Really? Why do they call it that?"

"I'll show you." She said, taking a huge swig from the bottle, throwing a pair of minute panties onto the bed beside him, and pulling her skirt up to her waist.

"Would you like some of this?"

"You know," said Winston thoughtfully, "I think I might."

27

The next morning the sky was leaden, with not the slightest sign of the sun's presence or of its imminent arrival. If one executed a painting of the scene, it could justly be entitled *Day Without Hope*. The dirty, dark grey clouds were so low it seemed as if one could reach up and touch them, although there was no clear reason why anyone would want to do it.

In the harbour, the wind, with force but no apparent hurry, swept across the surface of the greasy, grey-green water, brutally bashing it into large, rolling waves with dirty white foam and glassy, turquoise walls. Around the pilings at the wharf, their velocity reduced, the waves swirled endlessly, worrying items of detritus: cigarette packages, candy wrappers, plastic containers, bottle caps and used, sad, spent, deserted condoms.

Spots of cold rain began to spray from the charcoal sky as gulls and terns sat hunched on capstans, shifting from one leg to the other, their feathers ruffling in the breeze. A dog, whose fur arose in protest when it faced the wind, sniffed round a lamppost, its meagre light having since dissipated, and shook himself to shed the accumulated rain.

Obviously disappointed by the paucity of interesting items at the lamppost, the dog trotted miserably off to a large warehouse. There, it nosed in and out of coiled cables and stacked lobster traps.

Hearing a chorus of heavy breathing, coughing and spluttering from a large packing case, the animal cautiously poked its head around the edge of the receptacle. Inside, Lonnie Kelly was curled up like an ugly, unwashed fetus.

The dog barked gruffly, and Lonnie awakened, blinking furiously to adjust his eyes to the first light. He spat at the dog which, avoiding the projectile, wandered off along the side of the building.

~

About half a mile to the north, huddled against the rising wind, Donnie McNeil and his work mates trooped across the muddy Number Twenty–Six yard to the lamp house. Here they resolved themselves into a single file and shuffled past the lamp man. As they reached the grille, each called out his check number, and the lamp man pushed his equipment over the counter.

"Hello, Cruel World!" shouted Bernie Verbeski from Caledonia.

"Abandon Hope all ye who enter here," Sam Vokey said.

"Nice to start the day on a cheerful note," Donnie observed.

"And to think it's downhill all the way from here," Bucky Watkins, from the Sterling, said, slapping Donnie on the back. "But the good news is we get to do it all over again, tomorrow."

~

Back at the MacNeil house, it was very dark and very quiet, apart from Murdoch's snoring. Rita tip-toed around the kitchen, careful not to touch anything which would make a loud noise if it fell.

She silently filled the kettle from a barely-running tap, put it on the stove, lit the gas, and then went to the cupboard to get the tea. Red Rose it was. It was always Red Rose because Katie would allow no other brand in the house.

"Only in Canada, you say?" said Rita, quietly imitating an upper-class English person. Then, answering herself, she uttered, "Pity!"

Behind the tea can she saw Dorothy's letter propped up against the sugar. She took it down and re-read it until the kettle's low whistle startled her. She pulled the kettle off the ring, folded the letter and replaced it on the shelf.

Suddenly it struck her that there had been little or no discussion about the letter. That was very strange, she thought, as she was almost certain her father would not favour the letter's proposal, and would be loud and long in its denunciation.

Maybe her mother had not even apprised him of its arrival. If she had, surely, something like this must have been ventilated, she thought, unless the subject had come up when she had been away from the house. Unless....she stopped dead at the kitchen table. Unless they deliberately discussed it when she was not present.

So, that was it. She banged her mug on the table, knowing it might wake her parents.

"Fuck them!" she shouted.

~

Annie Pyke came downstairs, knowing Arthur would be sitting at the window as he always did. He had not shaved yet and was in his underpants and tee-shirt. She could easily tell he had been smoking from the, to her, disgusting smell, but she said nothing.

"Do you want me to make you anything, Dad? I got the time."

"No, no dear. I'll cook meself some bacon later on. I'll have it with some beans and toast."

"Well, I'll push off then."

"Aren't you gonna have somethin'?"

"I has my breffast at the café, you knows that."

"Ah yes. I forgot. See you later, alligator."

"In a while, crocodile."

Clutching at her raincoat with one hand and at its plastic hood with the other, Annie closed the door behind her and battled the wind to the gate. Often she walked the two kilometres to work, sometimes with her friend, Dolores Scott, who lived two rows away, but frequently she would get a ride with one of her neighbours.

Familiar with the way fate worked, Annie was supremely confident that, today, she would not see hide nor hair of a lift, and that she would get soaked to the skin. It was a good thing she kept a complete change of clothes at the Melody.

~

Looking warily about him, Winston teetered down the slippery, wet wooden stairs, skidded down the gravel driveway and tottered across to his car. Once inside, he drove back towards town and turned on to Wallace's Road, where he parked near St. Joseph's Hospital.

He took a battery-powered shaver from his glove compartment and proceeded to shave himself. Unlike many of his intimate adventures, he thought as he manoeuvred the razor, that one had been quite something, convincing him yet again that experience and practice were their own reward.

~

Across the street, on the second floor of St. Joseph's, Violet was asleep in a large armchair with a plaid blanket thrown over her. In a bed next to, Margie was also sleeping. She looked even paler than she had a day earlier and years older than her actual age. She was hooked up to various monitors and intravenous substances.

Outside the door to the room, Dr. Rajani, a surgeon, and Doctors

Tompkins and Khalifa, in hushed tones, discussed a report which the head nurse, Mrs Hemsworth, held in front of her.

"Could they do anything for her if we could move her to Halifax?" she asked.

"What could they do?" asked Rajani rhetorically.

"That's precisely that nub of it," Dr. Tompkins said. "Nothing. The best thing would be to get Violet's consent and then gradually withdraw the meds. Are we agreed?"

"Agreed," said Khalifa.

28

Rita sat at the kitchen table, sipping her tea. Above, Murdoch's snoring became louder, a sign that her mother would soon be down. Katie always said that lying in bed with Murdoch next to her was like trying to rest in a shed full of locomotives. Once she awoke, there was no point in her lingering between the sheets.

Rita wondered if she should introduce the subject of Dorothy's letter into the conversation. She knew that making accusations would get nowhere, but she thought she might just mention finding the letter, and see where it led.

"Morning Ma," she said as a bleary Katie tottered into the kitchen. "How are yez today?"

"Not too bad, girl. Himself woke me with his clatter...as usual. I was dreaming I was a little girl with my auntie out in the country. We was pickin' somethin'."

"What was you pickin'?"

"I don't know. If I did know I'd've told yez."

"I was only asking. I didn't mean nothin' by it."

"Maybe them little blue flowers. What're they called?"

"What's what called?"

"Them little blue flowers."

"What little blue flowers?"

"The ones I was pickin' in the dream."

"I thought you said you couldn't remember what you was pickin' in the dream."

"It just came back to me."

"Jesus! You gotta be a mind reader around this place."

"Watch your mouth, my girl," Katie snapped. She looked around the place, her gaze settling on the stove. "How long ago did you make that tea?"

""Bout half hour. It'll be some stewed now."

"Just about right, then." Katie got up, went to the stove and poured herself a cup.

"My God, thass as black as the wall in Ten North. Let me make some fresh, Ma."

"This'll do," Katie averred stoically.

"Oh, Ma."

"Yeah?"

"When I was getting the tea, I come across Dotty's letter..."

"Call her by her right name, damn you, her name is Dorothy!"

"Sorry, I saw the letter and I was wondering if you'd mentioned it to the old feller yet."

"No, I been waitin' for the right moment."

So, Rita thought, they had not discussed its contents behind her back, so there was no reason for her to harbour conspiracy theories. At least, not at this stage. However, she determined it was a developing situation she would have to monitor.

"D'you think there'll ever be a right moment with him?"

"No, I guess not. I'll do it today."

"Good luck with that."

"I'm gonna need it. What shift you on today?"

"I'm off today."

"What? Why?"

"I decided I deserved a day off."

"Hmmn. What you gonna do with it. It don't look like much of a day to me."

Rita got up from the table and went to the sink. She was not comfortable having this conversation with her mother because, while not exactly lying, she was not telling the whole truth. She also did not want Katie to get a good look at her face, which bore much more make-up than usual.

"I figured I'd go into Sydney. Do a bit of shoppin'. Maybe go see Sandra and Rosie."

"Ah. How're they gettin' along those days?"

"Don't know. That's why I thought I'd look them up."

To bring the conversation to an end, Rita turned the sink tap on full and vigorously began to wash her cup and saucer.

Soon the sound of her father moving about sent her flying from the room. She passed him on the stairs, her body momentarily touching his lumbering, larger, slightly smelly one. She shuddered, went to her room (or cell, as she sometimes described it), and put on her very best dress and brand new underwear. Katie had insisted that, as kids, they all wear clean underwear in case they had to go to hospital, but this went a step beyond sanitation, as she knew that if her mother could see these she would certainly disapprove.

She crept quietly downstairs and stopped for a minute outside the living room door.

"So that's what it's all about!" she heard her father shout. By the sounds emanating from inside, he was rampaging around the room. "I knew you were up to something, my girl. I just knew you had some Jeezly bee in your bonnet. I can read you like a goddamn book."

Holding her breath, Rita gently opened the front door, slipped out, closed it again, and dashed into the row. Had the gate been shut she was positive she would have flown over it.

With a quick look back over her shoulder, she ran down the row to where Gerald Tracey had promised to give her ride into town to the bus station.

She was free. More than that, she was a woman with a plan.

Back in the house, hostilities were ongoing with a renewed spirit and an increasing vigour. As Murdoch stalked up and down the living room, Katie had retreated behind the chesterfield for fear her husband might be carried away and verbal assaults might become physical.

"Don't you be bawlin' at me. You great brute!"

"I'll bawl at you as much as I want. How long was yez gonna keep it from me, you witch? If I hadn't heard you and our Rita hissin' and plottin', I don't doubt I would've been in the dark for days."

"What d'you mean you heard us? You was upstairs."

"Ah ha! You foolish old mare. Don't yez know that there's a hole in the corner? If you listens close enough yez can hear every word."

"What?" Katie looked to the ceiling where the presence of a dark hole confirmed Murdoch's claim. "Jesus! You been spyin' on me all these years, b'y."

"Most of the time I'm guessing what you says ain't worth hearing, but I was huntin' for them old slippers Marjorie give me for Christmas a few years back—on me hands and knees, I was—and thass when I heard you two schemin'."

"Of all the low, dirty tricks you ever stooped to, this is the lowest and the dirtiest."

"A good thing I did, thass all that I can say,"

Murdoch sat down, evidently satisfied he had the best of the argument. They glared at each other in silence for several minutes, neither wanting to be the one to break the truce, if that is what it was.

Finally Katie could stand it no longer. "Murdick, please just hear me out. It makes a lot of sense because we're neither of us getting' any younger, and four of our grandchildren are up there."

"Hmph!"

"I just want you to think on it."

"Out of the question!"

"Think about about me for a change. I'm sick of cookin' and cleaning. I'm an old woman, Murdick."

"If you ever got up there all yez'd be doin' is interferin' with Dorothy and tryin' to do her washing and cookin' and cleanin'. Wouldn't work. Believe me."

Katie had more vitriol in her reserve, but decided not to use it, and to try a softer approach. She bit her lip, came out from behind the couch and put her gnarled hand on his arm.

"What about our Donnie? Don't you think of him?"

"What the hell's he got to do with it? You plan on haulin' him up there by your apron strings?"

"No, 'course not, My God, Murdick, the older you get, the foolisher you get. I mean so's he and Annie could have the house. He's goin' on thirty and still single."

"Oh, I see. So he's in on this little conspiracy, too, is he? The little bastard can't wait to put his father out of his own house!"

"Oh, don't be so foolish! It's not like that, and you know it."

She scuttled to the doorway, but turned back to launch a final assault. "Are you too old and too stubborn that your brains is shrivelled up? All I'm asking is to think about it,"

"I ain't goin'! You hear me, you old witch? I ain't goin' and thass all there is to it! I ain't goin'! Thass an end on it!"

29

Rita walked through the wind and spotting rain until she came to the end of the row, turned right and continued to where West Avenue joined Centre Avenue. This is where she had arranged to meet Gerald Tracey, since he was coming from New Aberdeen. When she had quietly called him on the phone he had offered to pick her up at the house, but the last thing she wanted was gossiping people linking her with a much older, married man.

"You're looking some good today, Rita," Gerald said when she climbed into his car.

"Nothin' special," she replied in an off-hand manner, knowing it was untrue. "I'm just goin' into Sydney. Where'd you think I'm goin', to see the Queen of England?"

"Well, I don't think you'd be outa place at Buckingham Palace. I never seen you like that before. I didn't mean nothin' by it, Rita."

"I know, Gerald. Sorry. Thanks, b'y, for givin' me a ride."

"Think nothin' of it, girl. Oh, Jesus!"

"What's wrong?"

"Listen to that, will you?" Gerald said, alerting her to a loud clicking sound from under the hood. "It's that frigging alternator again!"

He steered the car to the edge of the street and turned off the ignition. They were on Sterling Road. "It's no good. I can't push it. It'll only give me a bigger bill to pay. I'll have to find a phone so I can call my service station. Freddie Burgoyne and Billy Chew always does my car."

"They on Union Street?"

"Yeah. They'll have to come up and tow me."

"Damn. I'll miss me bus."

"Awful sorry, Rita. What will you do?"

"Can't be hanging around for hours. I guess I'll have to get a taxi from the Post Office."

"That'll cost you some."

"Can't be helped," said Rita as she clambered out. "Good luck with the car."

She struck out down the road, her high heels making heavy weather of the journey. Damn and blast! Her bold plans for the day were already in partial ruins. She wondered if this was an omen, and whether she should simply turn back and go home.

Rita half believed in omens, often called fore-runners, as many people of Keltic ancestry did, and when the mood and light were right, she believed in ghosts, too. But although she had heard dozens of stories about people dying immediately following some sign or other, or of folk losing out on fortunes because they had not done what some psychic had told them, she had never seen absolute proof of any of it.

Today, she decided that, omens notwithstanding, she would not be stopped. She had taken over an hour to put on her make-up and select her clothes, and she was not going to allow the effort to go to waste.

Very soon she came to the junction with Minto Street. Many called this "Sneak Street", since it allowed a drunken man to leave the tavern and get home to the Sterling and New Aberdeen without passing the police station on MacKeen Street. Rita reflected that there were other contenders in Glace Bay for the sobriquet "Sneak Street", including Bell Street, Brodie Avenue and Beach Street, each with its own reasons.

For her purposes today, which were not avoiding detection but saving time, she turned into Minto and carried on in fine, spitting rain until she reached Main Street.

From there it was just a short walk past the Credit Union and the Cape Breton Post Building to the taxi rank in front of the impressive, redbrick, Edwardian Post Office.

Several taxis were available, all their drivers either sitting on or leaning against the wall, smoking and exchanging yarns. Most of them were elderly men, or miners in their fifties who had been "pre-retired" by the company.

Rita recognized one of them who was wiping down his new Chevy, and went up to him. He was Gordon Smith, town councillor for Ward Four and Deputy Mayor. Gordon had been a miner but had been incapacitated at a relatively early age by pneumonoconiosis, a lung disease caused by inhalation of coal dust.

"Morning, Mr. Smith."

"Good morning, Madam."

"I missed me bus and have to get to Sydney. How much would it cost?"

"Rita MacNeil, isn't it. From up The Hub?"

"Yeah, Thass me."

"I know your father and your mother. Good people."

"Thanks."

"Tell you what," he said, "give me five bucks, but not till we get in their car. I don't want any of these other guys to see."

Although she felt ill at ease in Gordon's car, she knew she would have been infinitely more uncomfortable on the bus. There, unless she nabbed the backseat, she would have been where all and sundry could have seen her, remarked on her appearance and, worst, "talked about" her afterwards with friends and acquaintances. She knew Gordon would not subject her to anything like that, as she was known as a gentleman.

Fortunately, he maintained a discreet silence for the entire journey. It was only broken when she heard Gordon wheezing and appearing distressed.

"Are you okay, Gordon?"

"It's just the black lung," he said hoarsely. "It's always worse in the damp weather."

The houses, in almost every colour of the rainbow, sped by. On Welton Street she noticed a sign on the front lawn of a house advertising *Shebib's Eczema Salve*.

"Where do you want me to drop you?" he asked as they drove in on Prince Street.

"Oh." Rita was not sure where she wanted to go. Her plan was only half formed; the part that pertained to the evening. For the rest of the day, she had only the vaguest notion. "Anywhere, Gordon. Thanks."

"How about I let you out on George Street?"

"That'd be fine. Thanks again."

She alighted and stood there as the taxi drove off. She looked about to get her bearings, noticing that the sun was finally attempting to break through the overcast cloud cover.

She had plenty of time, she told herself, and so she would just walk up and down the streets, looking in the windows, until it became necessary to make a move.

30

When Winston had finished shaving, he felt only a little better. Having awakened late, he had not been able to shower and, of course, he had been unable to have a change of clothes. While he may not have actually smelled rank, he knew he was unclean. The wages of sin might not immediately mean death, as St. Paul indicated to the Romans, but they certainly took their toll in other ways.

He thought of dashing into Sydney to have a thorough wash at his hotel, but realized it would take too much time as he was scheduled to meet Alex in an hour. Maybe a good breakfast and several cups of strong coffee might restore his strength and spirits.

Although he and Gloria had agreed to keep their assignation secret, as soon as he entered the Melody Café it quickly became apparent that she had never intended to keep her side of the bargain. She greeted him with looks, winks and a degree of enthusiasm which strongly suggested that some kind of liaison existed between them.

"Hi, there, handsome! How are you today? Better than yesterday, I'm guessing." She flashed a large, knowing smile.

Annoyed, Winston merely grunted and turned to Annie and Marlene, who were bustling forward to meet him.

"Good morning, ladies."

"Get on with your work, girls!" Annie snapped at her underlings. "Good morning, Winston. Just coffee, or are you here for breakfast?"

"Breakfast, please."

"Quite right. Bet that old hotel in Sydney don't give you a decent fry-up like we do."

"Er...right. You are so right, Annie. I'll have the works: eggs, sausage, bacon, home fries, toast, coffee—"

"No sooner said than done. Marlene! You heard that. Cook the man his food."

"Okay, Annie."

"Gloria! Clean out them toilets."

"I cleaned them only yesterday."

"Then clean them again!" Annie ordered as she slid into the booth across from Winston. "So, what have you got planned for today?"

"Alex is taking me to New Waterford to show me where a man was killed in 1925."

"That'd be William Davis."

"Yes, I think that's the name Alex said."

"How do you want your eggs, Mister?" Marlene called from the stove.

"Any way they come," Winston said.

"Sunny side up?"

"Sure."

Annie put her elbows on the table and allowed them to slide forward, bringing her closer to Winston.

"So, are you going to the Savoy tonight?"

"The Savoy. What's the Savoy?"

"It's just around the corner. The theatre."

"Ah, yes. I've seen it."

"Remember, I told you about the concert?"

"But it's Famous Players. Isn't it a movie house?"

"Yeah, but sometimes they uses the little stage part if anyone big is comin' to town."

"Oh yes. I'm sorry, it slipped my mind. What is it again?"

"John Allen Cameron."

"And is *he* big?"

"Around Cape Breton he sure is."

They were interrupted by Marlene bringing two coffees, and cutlery and a napkin for Winston.

"Tell me about him."

"He's from Inverness."

"Where's that?"

"About 100 miles due west from here."

"That's still on the island."

"I hope to tell you it is."

"What kind of entertainment does he provide?"

"He used to be a priest—"

"A priest? Is he going to say Mass at the concert?"

"No b'y." She giggled. "He sings the old sings—you likely wouldn't know them—and plays the guitar."

"Oh, I see."

"So, you'll be there?" Annie whispered.

Before she could say more, Marlene arrived with Winston's breakfast. "Do yez want toast?"

"Yes, please. Could I have brown?"

"Sure. I'll be right back with it."

"I got you the ticket just like I said I would." Annie said and pushed a small piece of cardboard across the table.

"Thank you."

"I'll see you outside at seven," she whispered. Then, rising she said loudly, "I'll see what's happening to your toast, b'y."

31

Winston picked Alex up outside his house, and they drove through Dominion and Gardiner Mines, and along the shore until they got to Scotchtown, on the outskirts of the town of New Waterford. He instructed Winston to turn left on Emerald Street, the dividing line between the two communities, and stop when he came to Heelan Street.

"Park anywhere round here, b'y."

"Right," said Winston, having found a place. "What now?"

"Get out. I think we oughta walk the rest of the way."

The day was considerably better than yesterday, with plenty of sunshine, but it was still extremely blustery. Clouds, birds, trees and bushes all seemed to be tossing wildly. They strolled back to the junction, and looked down Heelan Street.

"They must have come up here," said Alex, pulling his cap off in case the wind blew it away.

"Who did?"

"The men. In 1925."

"Oh, right. How many were there?"

"At least 2,000. Some say as many as 3,000."

"Where did they come from?"

"From down there. I'm after tellin' you. In Waterford."

"Yes, I know, but they must have assembled somewhere."

"I don't know. The main drag is Plummer Avenue. Or maybe they gathered at one of the pits."

"How many collieries were operating then?"

"Oh, lemme see. There would have been No. 12, No.14 and No, 16 in the town and No.17 on the edge of town in New Victoria. Twelve is still going today. It's up there away up on Ellsworth Avenue. Sixteen was just down the road here, on the left. It closed not too long ago."

"It's all very confusing, Alex—"

"Alec."

"Yes. So, we don't exactly know where the men assembled, but we know they came up here. Where did they go from where we are now?"

"Thass what I'm tellin' you. Follow me, b'y."

Winston followed Alex as they threaded their way through the neat streets and nicely tended houses of Scotchtown until they came to Daley Road.

"These here tracks," said Alex, pointing to some gleaming rails, "mark the boundary between Waterford and New Victoria, which is in the county."

"Where do they come from?"

"From Twelve pit."

"To where?"

"They goes all the way to the piers in Sydney. So the coal can be shipped out."

They walked on, then, taking a left turn, saw Waterford Lake ahead of them. Alex spread his arms to encompass the scene.

"So here's how it went: In March 1925, the company cut off credit at the company stores and held out from offering a deal with the union. So the miners took control of the power plant, and on June 11 a gang of company police—or 'goons', as the men called them—took it back. Thass what the march was all about. To go get the plant back under union control."

"This is where it happened. Where the man was shot?"

"There was three shot."

"Three killed?"

"No, three shot. Gil Watson and Jack MacQuarrie was injured but only Billy Davis was killed."

"Ah. Was that right here?"

"Here's the thing, Winston, nobody knows for sure. I heard where Billy's daughter—she still lives in town—said he wasn't part of the march. She said he went to the store to get a nipple for the baby's bottle and was caught in the crossfire."

"So if that was the case, he couldn't have been here at the Lake."

"I guess not, although most of the versions says he was."

"It makes for a better story that way."

"Don't be sayin' stuff like back in town." Alex frowned. "It wouldn't be pop'lar."

"Okay, I won't."

"So, to make a long story short, the men come marchin' up this road and the goons, who was on horseback, went up on the high sides and kind of trapped the men in the middle."

"What happened then?"

"They fell on them like a ton of bricks, b'y, beatin' at them with them baton things. 'Cause the men was unarmed, they tried to get away and hide in the woods if they could."

"That's when the goons started firing?"

"I guess so. I heard one feller sayin' that he had his little dog with him and the dog's nose was shot off."

"Ouch. What happened to the two who survived?"

"Watson and MacQuarrie? One was shot in the groin, I b'lieve—don't know if that put paid to his fatherin' kids—and the other took it in the stomach. They say Watson still had the bullet inside his gut when he died, years after."

"Well, thank you Alec. That was fascinating."

"Think there's a movie in this?"

"At least one, but it won't be my decision. Dan will make that de-cision, and the banks."

"What've they got to do with it?"

"No money, no movie. You wouldn't believe the hoops Dan will have to jump through to get a movie made. And the people who provide the money are the first who have to be convinced that the story is bankable."

"I never thought of it like that."

The wind had dropped now, so Alex put his cap back on. "Let's go back, b'y. We'll drive to the top of River Ryan Hill. From there we'll be able to see most of the county."

Winston did as Alex instructed him and soon they had pulled off the road and got out.

The sun was now hot and the sky was almost cloudless. To the left was Lingan Point, and beyond, the Atlantic Ocean, shimmering and sparkling like many trillion bright, new pins. To their right was mostly wooded land, broken by lighter green patches of the golf course, with Sydney some miles further on. Ahead of them, to the southeast, lay the communities of Glace Bay, Dominion and Re-serve Mines.

"Now then," said Alex as he rolled himself a cigarette while lean-ing against the car, "here's what you gotta understand, Winston. Near every pit there was a company store where the families got the groceries and clothes and stuff—"

"And the cost was deducted from their pay. Bill and Archie were telling us at the Pensioners' Union."

"Yeah, thass what I'm tellin' you b'y. So in 1925 there would've been pluck-mes at—"

"Pluck-mes?"

"Thass what they called the company stores."

"Oh, right."

"Anyways, there would've been one way over at Donkin—that'd

be for Number 6. Ahead there, the first you would come to in Glace Bay would be Number 1B, which is where Number 26 is today. Then Number 2—thass the one in New Aberdeen, where Number 20 is now."

Alex moved his extended arm and pointed. "Number 4 in Caledonia. And up a bit to the right from that, Number 11 in Passchendaele. Then, further to the right there, at Reserve—for Number 5 and Number 10"

"By my calculations, including the ones in the New Waterford area—which are behind us—there would have been twelve collieries working at that time and a company store for each one." Winston said, his brow furrowing. "Does that sound right?"

"Yeah, that sounds about right."

"So what happened to them?"

"Woosh!"

"Woosh?"

"They all went up in smoke. In one night. Over on the Northside in Sydney Mines, too."

"Holy cow! I guess we know who was responsible?"

"Some say company agents fired their own stores—"

"Why would they do that?"

"'Cause everyone would think the men done it, and the strike would lose support."

"Is that true?"

"I don't know, b'y. It's more likely the men burned them down in their anger with the company."

"Hmm."

"That's somethin' else you shouldn't question when we're back in town."

32

As Rita wandered around the streets of Sydney, she realized that she had never been here before except in the company of others. She thought that she could probably count her total number of visits on two hands, and in every case she had either younger siblings gadding around her, or her mother nagging her to stand up straight and dragging her away from shop windows.

Today she was resolved to do as much window-shopping as she felt inclined to do, and not one window fewer. She roughly calculated the number of shops on Charlotte Street and divided the estimated length of her visit by that number. If a store window was particularly uninteresting she would spend less time in front of it, but would add the surplus gained to the next attractive window. It did not matter what a store's specialty was; Rita bestowed time upon it and gave each one a critical examination.

She passed by Chernin's Men's Wear, where proprietor Isaac was standing in the doorway. She crossed over and looked into the Napoli Pizzeria, where she watched Francesco Dellorusso twirl the dough around and throw it so high it almost hit the ceiling. Further on, she noted with a pang of excitement that *Love Story* was playing at the Vogue movie house.

Close by was Hal's Pawn shop, with so many intriguing items on display that she overran her time limit and had to deduct some minutes from other windows.

Next was Ike's Delicatessen with its strange and lovely smells.

She peered in and saw Ike and Faye bustling about, laying out exotic foods Rita had never eaten, and probably never would.

Then the London Grill, featuring a new sensation, Kentucky fried chicken. This was considered a very posh place, where Rita had never dined. She looked through the curtained windows and saw tables gaily spread with gingham cloths and the smartly dressed waitresses in gingham dresses. She wondered why Kentucky chicken was different from other chicken, what it tasted like, and what Grecian bread was.

Rita paused and felt again the wad of money in her raincoat. She had withdrawn most of her meagre savings from the Credit Union. She knew she was going to disperse most, if not all, of the money today, but had only semi-formed notions of how it would be expended.

The London Grill looked enticing and she toyed with the idea of coming here for lunch, or maybe supper.

After a few minutes Rita decided that Kentucky chicken would have to wait until another occasion. She ambled on up Charlotte Street, spending more than the allotted time eyeing the diamond rings and necklaces in Alteen's Jewellers, and the lovely dresses in the Smart Shop.

A notice in the Diana Sweets window advised her that hot sandwiches came with fries and gravy, and were available in all four meats. Rita's brow furrowed. She could figure out beef, pork and chicken without any difficulty, but could not think what the fourth meat could be. She considered going in and asking, but could not summon up the necessary courage.

So Rita wiled away most of the day and loved every minute of it. There was no-one to rag her and nobody to nag her. She was free and had money in her pocket. Even the sun was on her side, and had now changed what had started as a desperately gloomy day into one of brightness and promise.

Promise: The very word made her pulse race, and the feeling of expectation welled up just below her sternum. How would this day end? She asked herself this question almost every few minutes and, more than once, she considered dismissing her dreams as foolishness and taking the bus back to Glace Bay.

Suddenly, Rita found that she was again in front of the Smart Shop. Had she lost her bearings, or was fate playing its part? She took a deep breath and, pulling back her shoulders, opened the door and went in. Don't seem nervous or insecure, she told herself. If a customer seemed intimidated, she had been told by Sheila Hillier, who worked in a garment store, the staff will look down at you and "fob you off with garbage."

"Good day, Madam," Proprietor Harvey Webber said, smiling.

"I want to see some dresses," said Rita imperiously and, she feared, rather rudely.

"Certainly, Madam. Mrs. Rudderham!" he called to a stout, middle-aged woman at the back of the store. "Please to show this lady some dresses."

"Yes, Mr. Webber," she said. "Follow me, dear. We'll fix you up. Is that daytime dresses or evening dresses?"

This took Rita by surprise as it had not occurred to her that there was a difference except for movie stars and the "mucky mucks". She made the split-second decision based on the fact that she intended to wear it that evening.

"Evening."

"We've got some lovely evening dresses, dear. Come this way."

Rita was forced to vigorously shake her head at the first four dresses laid out before her on account of their prohibitive price. Then Mrs. Rudderham brought out three more which, while still ridiculously expensive, were just within Rita's means.

She rejected one of these because it was an emerald green, a colour she detested. That left a dark blue dress with a slight silver streak in the fabric, and a lighter blue with delicate white flowers. She tried each of them on and they fitted perfectly. Not needing alterations was a huge plus.

She loved them both but loved the light blue dress with a childish passion. The problem was that while both dresses were low cut, and her mother would describe both as "shameful", Katie would say that the light blue one was "jail bait." Rita's heart was pounding and her courage was beginning to fade.

"What do you think?" she asked Mrs. Rudderham.

"They're both beautiful."

"Do you think this one is too…."

"Too what, dear?"

"Too…er…revealin'?"

"Ah, too sexy?"

"Yes."

"Actually no, dear. The dark blue one is extremely sexy, but in an adult way."

"Alright, I'll take it. Will you wrap it up for me, please?"

"Of course I will, dear. What a funny question to ask."

Precious parcel under her arm, Rita proceeded up Charlotte until she spotted a ladies' hairdresser just around the corner on Pitt Street.

She went in and a woman called Joan ushered her to a large padded chair.

"What'll it be?" Joan asked.

"You'll get a laugh out of this," said Rita, "but I wants you to make me look beautiful."

"You're not too shabby the way you are, but leave yourself in my hands."

"Thanks."

"How long have you got?"

"As long as it don't go beyond supper time, as long as you like."

"Okay, but it won't be cheap."

"That's no problem," Rita said, although she had already spent the lion's share of her money on the dress.

She lay back in the chair, closed her eyes and went to sleep. She dreamed of crowds chasing her, wearing the blue dress, up Commercial Street and throwing stones at her. "Floozy! Bike! Whore!" they shouted as she tore up Sneak Street and up into the Sterling.

There she climbed into the back of a Mail Van. Eddie Butts was driving, saying over his shoulder, "You're all mine now, girl!"

"Just take a look at that." The sound of Joan's voice brought her back to reality.

Joan had done a marvellous job. Rita could scarcely believe that the woman in the mirror was herself. It took her breath away, but also scared her. She knew it bought her one step closer to the point of no return.

When she reappeared on the street, it was late afternoon. She was looking and feeling like a totally different person.

She turned into Dorchester Street and walked towards the Esplanade until she found a café on the left-hand side. The place was empty and a man, presumably the proprietor, was washing down some tables.

"How do?" said the man.

"Hi. I'm gonna order somethin' for me supper, but could I go to the washroom first?"

"Sure."

"I wants to wash and change outa me work clothes."

"Fine. You don't have to tell me your life story," the man said with a huge smile. "I'm Cecil, by the way."

"Thanks, Cecil."

Sometime later, when she emerged from the washroom, she was completely transformed.

Cecil did a double take, thinking at first it was another customer.

"My God, lady. You look like you just stepped out of a movie."

"G'way, b'y," Rita said, embarrassed. "What do you recommend for supper, Cecil?"

"Burger and fries'd be good."

"Nah, too messy. I might get grease'n stuff on me new dress."

"I got a nice bit of cod. Would you like that with some mashed potatoes and carrots?"

"Lovely."

Rita went to the table in the centre of the window and sat down facing out. She put the parcel containing her old clothes on the chair beside her, and exchanged small talk with Cecil while he cooked her dinner.

When he put the food in front of her, it looked excellent and Rita ate it with pleasure. Then she had a piece of pie with a cup of coffee. Then she got up and headed back to the washroom.

"Cecil, you don't mind if I hang around her for a while, do you?

"Help yourself. I don't expect a whole lot of customers tonight."

In the washroom, Rita's hand was shaking so much she could hardly clean her teeth with the brush she had brought from home. But she persevered and the task done, she returned to her table.

From where she sat she had a clear view of the Isle Royale Hotel.

33

Katie MacNeil was on the telephone to Dorothy in Toronto. When she wanted to speak to her daughter, they had a code to ensure that all calls were paid for by Tom, Dorothy's husband. Katie would let the phone ring twice, hang up, then repeat the process once. Then Dorothy would call her back.

It could not be fairly said that Katie actually abused this procedure, but Dorothy thought that her mother used it for matters which were not of paramount importance.

More than once, Tom had looked up from paying the monthly bills to comment, ostensibly to himself, but loud enough for others to hear, "Hmmm. Another call to Glace Bay, Nova Scotia. Four dollars and fifty three cents. And another for five dollars and twenty three cents. And what have we here? Good Lord, what a surprise! Glace Bay, Nova Scotia, seven dollars and forty-one cents. What on earth could the people have to say to keep them on the line that long? Guess we'll never know."

Dorothy heard all these *sotto voce* remarks, but acknowledged none of them, preferring to continue to read or watch television or peel vegetables as though nothing had been said. But it *did* bother her and as a result she was sometimes annoyed when Katie called to discuss trivial matters.

However, The subject of today's call was not a trivial matter to either mother or daughter,.

"He's gone down to the hospital to see little Margie—you know, the one that lives across the road. Violet's child—so I thought I should call you while he's out."

"Smart thinking, Ma. What progress are you making? Any?"

"Not so good, so far, Dorothy, but I'm not giving up. No, sir, I ain't."

"How long do you think it might take you to bring him around? Tom and me got to make plans. We can't wait forever."

"It's hard to say, dear. You know what he's like. Maybe sooner, maybe later."

"Look, Ma, if it's gonna be that much trouble, maybe it wasn't such a good idea after all."

"No, no. I'll bring him around. You see if I don't. Don't you worry about that, my girl."

"Alright. Keep me posted."

"You better b'lieve I will."

"Oh, Ma?"

"Yeah?"

"Just not too often, huh? I won't be wantin' an update every day."

~

As his wife and daughter were talking about him behind his back, Murdoch was sitting with Violet by Margie's bedside at St, Joseph's Hospital. The little girl looked white and drawn. In her surgical cap she seemed very old.

"I sure would miss you, if you went away to live, Murdick," said Violet.

"I know you would. I ain't gone yet."

"I wish I could also say"—Violet dropped her voice to a whisper even though it was clear that Margie was unconscious—"that Margie will miss you, too. But it don't look like she's gonna be around much longer."

"I'm gonna miss my daily walks with her, for sure. But even with her gone, I'd miss you, Violet. Thass one of the reasons I don't want to go any place."

"You're some kind, Murdick."

~

At that moment, Winston and Alex MacDonald were driving along Main Street, when suddenly Lonnie Kelly lurched in front of them. Winston was able to veer the car enough to avoid hitting the man, and for his pains was rewarded by a fearsome glower from Kelly.

"My God, Alex, he's one evil-looking bastard. He seems to crop up all over the place. Everywhere I go, I see him."

"He's ugly, that's for sure. And right fuckin' cantankerous with it, but I ain't sure there's much harm in him."

"Really? I'll take your word for it. How old is he?"

"Lemme see. He'd be about thirty now."

"Wow. He looks a lot older than that."

"Yeah, I guess the meths or whatever he drinks has pretty much fucked his liver."

"And his brain, too."

"I shouldn't wonder."

"Where now?"

"Turn right on Commercial Street and keep goin'. I thought we should take a look at the Miners' Museum."

"I didn't know they had one," said Winston. "It sounds interesting."

~

It was the slow period at the Melody Café. After the lunch time rush there had not been a customer for over half an hour. Gloria and Marlene were wiping down tables. Annie was titivating herself in the washroom in preparation for some shopping.

Eventually she emerged, her makeup clearly having been renewed. "I won't be gone long. Less than an hour. Can you handle things while I'm away?"

"Sure," said Gloria.

"Oh yes, Annie," Marlene said.

"See you stay outta trouble."

"Yeah okay Annie," Gloria said roguishly. "We won't steal the knives and forks or nothin'."

"Well, just see you don't!" Annie glared at her assistant and left the café.

No sooner had she taken a few steps down the street than Winston and Alex came round the corner. The men waved to her flamboyantly, but Annie merely inclined her head and smiled.

"Has she gone yet?" Gloria asked in a few minutes.

"Yeah, I see her goin' past Knox Church."

"Good. The bossy old cow!"

Marlene tripped over to where Gloria was standing, wide-eyed with anticipation. "Well?"

"Well what?"

"You knows what."

"No, I don't know what, if you don't say what you mean."

"You know. Last night. Did you see him last night?"

"See who?"

"Oh, come on, Gloria! I mean that Winston."

"What if I did?"

"So, you did see him!"

"Maybe, I can't remember."

"By the jumpin's, you'd better tell me or I'll—"

"Just what would you do, Marlene MacKinnon?"

"Aw, tell me, pleeeeeze, Gloria."

"I told you," said Gloria, suddenly becoming both friendly and conspiratorial. She put her face close to Marlene's. "I told you I'd have that fella before she would, and I did."

"Oh my!" Marlene gasped. "But you didn't…do…you know… *that*?"

"'Course I did. It was some nice, too."

"Oh my. Where?"

"My place. We did it a coupla times."

"Oooh! Gloria Maddin, you are bad. Downright wicked, b'y."

"No I ain't. I'm just having a good time. I'm entitled."

"My Lord. A man older than you. Older than your father, I shouldn't wonder. Some bad."

"You're only jealous," Gloria said, smiling and shrugging her shoulders.

~

Winston and Alex went down underneath the Miners' Museum to the Ocean Deeps Colliery, which partially simulated conditions in a real coal mine. Here they encountered a group of tourists and their old acquaintance, Danny the Dancer, who was one of the guides.

"Hang back, b'y," Alex said as soon as they saw Dancer. "Let's listen to what he's telling them American tourists."

There were about half a dozen people in front of them, so Winston and Alex were able to lurk unseen.

"How old were you when you went into the pit?" asked one woman.

"Nine years old!" declared Dancer. 'They plucked me from my mother's breast and hurled me into the bowels of the earth!"

"Is that true?" Winston whispered.

"I doubt it," Alex replied with a huge grin. "You'll see. He'll get a big tip from that woman later."

"Why did you have to go to work so young?" asked a teenage girl.

"Economic compulsion!" Dancer cried. "Work or starve. Man or boy. My lungs was ravaged. My growth was stunted…"

"He don't look too stunted to me," Alex hissed.

"No he certainly doesn't," Winston muttered.

"My education was blighted! Economic compulsion in the service of the capitalist system!"

"Tell us about the great strike," another tourist urged.

"They sent the dragoons of hell against us, the battalions of the devil, and we stared into the bayonets and down the gun barrels of the denizens of evil!"

Dancer was in high gear, producing gasps from his listeners. He wrapped up his peroration with a great flourish, graciously bowing and thanking the visitors for their donations, which he pocketed. Winston noted that one such contribution, from the woman Alex had predicted would give, was an American twenty-dollar bill.

When Dancer noticed their presence, he gave them a wink. They waved to him and drifted off.

Alex explained that this mine simulated Number 24 colliery, known as "The Victory", which had been located about a quarter of a mile to the south of where they stood. This was a slope mine opened in 1919 from the outcrop of the Emery Seam at Big Glace Bay Lake. The mine, which was originally interconnected with Number 11, was closed in 1953 because of the high transportation cost of the coal. Winston was astonished to learn that, at the time of closure, the distance from coal face to surface was four miles.

In the museum they studied the photographs on display. One was of a small boy amid a group of miners.

"That kid can't be much older than ten," Winston said.

"I guess not."

"So Dancer could be right?"

"You figure it out. The picture was taken in 1890. Dancer woulda been born in somethin' like 1905. If he's telling the truth he woulda hada gone down the pit in 1914."

"So it's not likely?"

"No b'y. Wasn't till 1923 the law said you hadda be 16, but before than the law was ten with restrictions on the hours worked."

"When was that passed?"

"In 1873."

"So, unless Dancer is a lot older than he looks, I guess he was embellishing the truth."

"I like that word, Winston. Embellishing. I must remember that one."

They wandered back to Winston's car. The afternoon was drawing on and a shift in the wind made it somewhat colder.

"What d'you wanna do now, b'y?"

"I'd like to do some writing, so I think I'll head back to Sydney, if you don't mind."

"No, I don't mind if you can take me back to the Hub."

On Main Street they saw Murdoch coming out of the Pensioners' Union, where he had gone after visiting the hospital. Winston slowed down and pulled up alongside him.

"Do you want a ride Murdick?"

"Sure, if there's any room in that sardine can."

"I guess we can squeeze you in somehow."

Alex got out, flipped back the seat to let Murdoch struggle into the rear space, where for a second he seemed to be stuck.

Alex put his hand on Murdoch's rump and gave him a push. "My God, you're gettin' some bulky in your old age, b'y."

"Thass all muscle, that is. All muscle."

34

Winston dropped Murdoch and Alex off in The Hub and drove off for Sydney. The two residents waved him farewell and each headed for his own gate.

"Don't go in right away, Alec. Have you got a few minutes to spare?"

"Sure. What's up, Murdick?"

"Walk over to the cliff with me. I got somethin' I wants to chew over with you."

"Alright. I hope nothin's wrong."

"Not exactly, no." Murdoch ran his hand through what little hair he had left. "Let's go and sit on that big rock."

"The tide's out. So, why not? Mind, the seaweed can be right slippy. So watch where you put your feet."

"Listen b'y, I was slippin' on that rock before you was born."

The evening was settling in, with a soft breeze and a kind light. The pinpricks of silver on a bright blue sea had merged into a mantle of shimmering coins as the water became greener and calmer. Visibility was almost perfect, South Head being clear and pronounced. Gulls which had earlier been squawking and chasing about the place, were now lazily cruising the azure sky.

Murdoch took a deep breath and told Alex all about Dorothy's proposal, the atmosphere it had produced and where matters stood at the present.

"I don't know what to say, Murdick. If your mind is made up, then it's made up."

"But do you think I'm being selfish?"

"How do you mean?"

"Am I being fair to Katie, do you think?"

"It ain't for me to say, b'y. I mean, if it's physically impossible for you to live in T'ronto, that's the end of the story."

"Do I owe it to her somehow?"

"Jesus, Murdick, you're asking questions which is none of my business to answer. I guess each of yez owes the other somethin', that's for sure, but what and how much only you twos can say."

"Hmm."

"Here's what I think if you really want to know. The least you can do is to go through the motions of giving it some thought. That way, your final decision might not hurt her so much."

"Thanks. It's gettin' a mite cold. Let's go in."

When Murdoch came into the house, Donnie was sprawled on the chesterfield, smoking and watching Bill Jessome reading the news on television. His first reaction was one of resentment at the thought of Donnie and Katie ganging up on him, but in his newly-determined amenable state, he told himself he would not cause trouble.

"There you are. How's she goin', b'y?"

"Good, b'y," said Donnie without looking up. "How's yourself?"

"Oh, you knows, up and down. I was in to see little Margie at the hospital. It's a sad business alright. Looks like she's fadin' fast."

'Aw, thass too bad. Did they put a time on it?"

"How do you mean?"

"Did they say how long she's got left?"

"Oh, no, but I think it's days rather than weeks."

He sat down, picked up the *Cape Breton Post* and idly scanned the headlines.

"A little bird tells me you'n Annie might be gettin' married."

Donnie immediately sat up, alert, but unsure as to which way the wind was blowing. In this house, he thought, the slightest word could be a trap to get you to dig a huge hole for yourself. He figured he had to pick his words carefully.

"Uh? Oh, yeah. Well, you know, sooner or later, I guess."

"Uh-huh."

"I can't put it off forever."

"I guess not. Well, I guess you know what you're doin'."

Donnie waited for his father to say more, to reveal more of how the land lay, but Murdoch continued to read in silence.

Frustrated, Donnie turned back to the television, where Bill Holmes was giving the results of harness racing at Blue Bonnets in Montreal. He shifted position, but could not get comfortable again.

"Hey, Ma! Any sign of supper yet?" he bawled in the direction of the kitchen.

Murdoch peered over the edge of his newspaper as Katie came bustling into the room.

"It's been on the table a while, b'y." she said.

"Then why didn't you tell us?"

"Watch how you talk to your mother," Murdoch growled.

"It's there. Yez can have it any time you want," Katie said tartly, her nose in the air.

Their antennae alerted and bristling, Murdoch and Donnie frowned and looked at each other. Each could tell something was up, but they did not know what.

Meekly they filed into the kitchen. On the table was a loaf of bread, a dish of butter, a chunk of rather elderly, orange cheese on a plate and an opened can of processed meat. The men's eyes flitted over the table then anxiously moved to the stove. The top was bare and the control lights were out, indicating the absence of any comestible in the oven.

"What's goin' on, Katie? Are you not feelin' good or somethin'?"

Murdoch said.

"I'm fine for an old woman. Just the usual aches and pains."

"Is this what's for supper? Nothin' cooked?" Donnie whined.

"What you see is what you gets. I got better things to do with what little time I got left in my old life to be slaving my fingers to the bone for ungrateful men."

Murdoch could believe neither his ears nor eyes. In all the decades they had been married, Katie had never done anything like this before. When the power had been lost a few times during winter storms, there had been no choice but to eat cold food, but no such excuse existed now. He stood there, his blood pressure rising, his eyes popping, and his temper climbing to boiling point.

"Goddamn you, woman!" he snarled. "This is nothin' but blackmail! And 'cause I wouldn't go along with your jeezly fool idea to go to our Dorothy's. So the plan is until I agrees, yez are plannin' to starve us!"

"Starve! Is that what you call good, nourishing food, is it? I guess if yez won't eat it, yez couldn't be very hungry in the first place."

"Jesus, Ma. Be reasonable." Donnie pleaded.

"And you can shut your mouth, too, you little Christer. You're a part and parcel of this goddamn foolishness. Don't think I don't know what's goin' on around here."

"Now, Murdick, don't be gettin' your blood pressure up—"

"You crazy old fool!" Murdoch grabbed the can of meat and hurled it at the garbage container in the corner. "You stupid, mischievous old fool! I come in here tonight ready to hear you out about Dorothy's idea, to see if there's some way it could be worked out. And what d'you do? You go and pull a stunt like this. Well, to hell with that! And to hell with you! I sure ain't goin' to be changin' my mind now!"

He stomped to the door, through the living room and, pausing only to grab the newspaper, raged out of the house and slammed the front door behind him.

Katie, her upper lip trembling and a tear running down her cheek, looked at Donnie.

"Nice one, Ma. You really handled that good, didn't you?"

"Well, what in the name of time was I s'pposed to do? I didn't know the stubborn old fool was weakening, did I?"

"Now it'll take three times as long to bring him round, if he ever does come round. Yez'd better be nice to him from here on in. Thass the only chance we got."

"Be nice to that cranky old bear? Like hell I will!"

Donnie glared at his mother, then sneered with a mixture of pity and contempt.

She collapsed onto a chair and started to cry. She was still crying when, a few minutes later, she heard the front door slam a second time.

~

Donnie strode away down the row towards town and the tavern. Meanwhile, Murdoch had taken refuge next door in the MacDonald house, which was a mirror image of his own, but not as well or as fully furnished. Here, too, holy pictures adorned the walls, but there were more of them, including one in which Christ was pictured with dark skin.

Alex and Evangeline sat on a moth-eaten couch while Murdoch occupied a large, reclining chair from which he unburdened himself of all his grievances.

"Holy God, b'y, sounds like you had a real donnybrook over there. We could hear you hollerin' through the wall, couldn't we, Ma?"

"Indeed we could," said the old lady, looking mortified.

"Yeah, I guess I lost my rag," Murdoch confessed sheepishly.

"You know, Murdick, I ain't takin' sides or nothin', but dat Katie is one good woman. You know dat? I knowed her goin' on fifty years and I know dat she's a good woman."

"Thass true, Murdick," said Alex. "You can't deny it."

Murdoch did not deny it, nor did he affirm it. He sat silent, looking at his hands, which he kept folded in his lap.

"I bet you couldn't find a better woman anywheres around here," Evangeline pronounced emphatically.

Murdoch grunted, half in recognition of an evident truth, half in annoyance that these people, to whom he had gone for succour, should remind him of it. He rose heavily and made for the door.

"Thanks, missus. Thanks, Alec. Reckon I'll be goin'."

35

Only two other customers came into the restaurant while Rita was waiting. One had fish and chips and a coke, while the other a hot pork sandwich, gravy and a coffee. Several times Rita looked at Cecil in an apologetic way, but he just smiled and shrugged.

Finally he came over to her table. "Listen, dear, it's okay. So long as I don't need your table for someone else, you can stay as long as you want. Makes no difference to me."

"Thanks, Cecil. I'm sorry to be such a pain."

"Are you waiting for a train or a bus?"

"No."

"Maybe you don't have anywhere to stay tonight. Is that it? I can call the Sally Ann. I'm sure we can fix you up with somethin'."

"No, no. It's nothin' like that." Rita laughed. "It's just that I'm waitin' for someone to get back to the hotel."

"Ah. I thought you wasn't no waif or stray. Will they be on foot or comin' in a car."

"A car."

"Right. And you would recognize it okay?"

"Oh yes. I would rec'onize it, alright."

"Then I'll leave you in peace. Want another hot coffee?"

"No, thanks."

Cecil went back behind his counter and fussily rearranged some squares and cakes in a glass case. The clock above his head showed Rita that over an hour had passed since she had finished her meal.

The sky was clouding over and it was starting to get dark.

She wondered if he had stopped for supper again somewhere in Glace Bay, as he had at her house quite recently. In that case, she reckoned, it might be another hour—or more—before he got back to Sydney. Worse, she thought with a sharp pang that afflicted her right below her sternum—he might be staying the night in Glace Bay. With a woman. Of course, that was it. That had to be it. Why did she not think of that before? It was the most logical course of events, and one she should have considered from the very outset.

Hating herself for her stupidity, she made up her mind to go straight back to Glace Bay and forget about this entire foolish venture.

Just as she was gathering up her parcels from the other chairs, she saw Winston's car pass by the window and drive round to the hotel parking lot. Her chest was thumping so hard she was afraid Cecil could hear it as she watched Winston saunter back and enter the hotel lobby.

"Thanks for everything, Cecil!" She called.

"Wait a minute!"

"What?"

"You didn't pay."

"Oh, my God, whatever was I thinkin' of? Here you are." She pushed a note into his hand. "Keep the change, b'y."

"Are you sure?" Cecil asked, amazed at his good luck. "All this?"

"You've been a real friend, Cecil. Just when I needed one."

Gingerly, Rita crossed the street, paused by the big glass doors, and swiftly cast her eye around the lobby. Years later, when she related her story to a friend, she described it, with a giggle, as "casing the joint."

She had seen how it was done in several movies and TV shows, and knew its success depended upon the desk clerk being the only employee in the lobby at the time. If there were more than one, she would have either turned round and left, pretending to have forgotten something, or taken a seat out of the clerk's line of vision.

When she saw a bellboy walking away from the desk, she decided her moment had come. She pushed through the doors and walked quickly to the desk.

"I have a package for Winston Barber," she said as officiously as she could, one hand conspicuously in her purse, "can you tell me what room he is in?"

"We can't give out that information, Miss. I'll get someone to deliver it for you."

He stepped out from behind the desk and looked around.

"It's very urgent. Time sensitive." She had also got that phrase from the television.

"Oh, alright," said the clerk, seeing no help in sight. "You'd better take it up yourself. Room 318."

"Thank you," she said and, seeing an elevator about to ascend, dashed forward and squeezed herself inside.

Winston's room was more of a small suite, with a bedroom opening out into a small sitting room with a sink, minuscule fridge, armchair, minute table and a tiny desk. He had just settled down to his typing and so far had written:

```
Town with Hope: A Treatment


Glace Bay is like a town which time has
forgotten. It sits on the brink of slip-
ping back, not into its immediate past of
busy industry and high employment, but
into its distant past when some fishing
boats and a few shacks existed alongside
the tepees of poverty-stricken....
```

There was a knock on the door, at first so timid that Winston thought it must have been to the adjacent room. He continued to type.

```
...indians of the local MicMac tribe. That
was before coal was discovered in commer-
cial quantities....
```

Another knock, this time louder, convinced him that it was indeed his door which was being rapped, so he rose, walked over and opened it, expecting to see a maid or bellhop.

"Hi, there. How's she goin'?"

Winston was stunned to see a woman, a rather beautiful woman, standing in front of him. He gaped in disbelief. "Rita? Is that you?"

"Well, it's not the Queen, that's for sure." She giggled nervously.

"What are you doing here?"

"I come to see you,"

"Uh...well, come on in."

Rita hesitated for a second, then slowly stepped forward. Even then, she stopped after proceeding a few inches, at which point she was neither in nor out of the room. This, she told herself, was what movies and novels called "the point of no return". She could mutter her apologies, swiftly whirl around and make a run for it. But one step further and there would be no going back. She would, in the words of her late Granny, be in for a penny, in for a pound.

She took a deep breath, momentarily closed her eyes, and...she was in the room.

"So, this is where you hang out," she burbled.

"Rita, you look—"

"Different? I know."

"No. Yes. I mean you look fabulous."

"Thanks. Can I put my stuff somewhere?"

Oh, Jesus, she thought, he thinks I look fabulous!

"Sure. Let me have it."

Winston moved quickly to relieve her of her bag and parcels, and carefully put them in the armchair. He turned back to find her awkwardly wringing her hands and weakly smiling. Both were temporarily lost for words as they stared at one another.

Embarrassed, she walked to the window and looked out at Dorchester Street "You got a great view," she said, knowing it was stupidly false.

"You're joking?"

"Yeah."

"So…"

"Listen, Winston, I was in Sydney anyway and I kind of wondered if you might be here." The words came pouring out, tumbling over themselves, persistent and unstoppable. "I remembered you tellin' me where you was stayin', so I figured I'd see if you were here. I mean, I just had supper across the street, but if you wanted to go someplace to eat, I'd be willin' to go with you. You know, if you didn't have plans or anythin'. Maybe you already ate and—"

"Rita! Slow down, please."

"I shouldn't have come. I know I shouldn't have come."

"No. I'm very glad you did."

"You are?"

"Yes."

"I won't stay long," she said. She thought, but did not say, I will stay here as long as you want, however long that may be, and I hope you want me to stay a long, long time.

"Jesus! I feel such a fool!" she cried, turning towards the door.

"Rita, what's wrong?"

Winston took her gently by the shoulders and pivoted her to face him. She was now sobbing and shaking, but despite her eyes being red and tears trickling down her face, Winston thought she looked so beautiful, so appealing. He took out a handkerchief and dabbed her face.

She gazed up at him, and then frowned. "Oh damnation!" she howled.

"What now?"

"With all the nerves and cryin' and everythin', I need to go to the toilet. Ain't that pathetic?"

"No, it's not pathetic. It's through that door there."

She made a dash for the bathroom, for refuge, and locked the door.

As she sat on the toilet, she thought that maybe fate had given her another chance to abandon her plan, to escape. Yes, she thought, that was it. Or, maybe, she had been given a chance to collect her thoughts and carefully formulate her declaration.

When she opened the bathroom door she had still not decided which course to follow. She took one look at Winston, smiling, tall, handsome and nice, and rushed at him, grabbing his hands.

"I want you so much, Winston. I'm 39 years old and only been with one other feller in my whole life until now. But God knows I wants you to be the second. Do you think I'm a fool?"

"No, I don't think you're a fool."

"I guess you think I'm cheap, like a whore or somethin'."

"No, no."

He pulled her to him and wrapped his arms around her. He bent his head and softly kissed her.

"Oh, my God," she moaned. "You don't know how long I've wanted you to do that."

Suddenly there was a loud rapping on the door. She leapt away from him, experiencing fear and surprise in equal measure. Could it be her father? Worse, her mother? Or the police?

"Who the Jesus is that?"

"It's room service. I ordered some food just before you arrived."

"Mother of God, I'm a bag of friggin' nerves."

"Why don't you sit down while I attend to this?"

Winston went to the door, took the tray from the bellhop and gave him one of those strange brown and red Canadian two dollar bills. Until he had been corrected, he had thought that they were fake, play money belonging to a board game.

He dragged up the small table with his foot and laid the tray on top. He had ordered a bottle of wine and a filet steak with mushrooms and fries.

"Do you want some of this, Rita?"

"No, thanks. I had haddock and potatoes across the road earlier."

"Why don't I cut off a corner of the steak and you can nibble it?"

"Okay," Rita giggled. "Could I have some of your wine, too?"

"Sure. It's Beaujolais. Do you know it?"

"What I knows about wine you could write on the back of a postage stamp."

"You'll like it," Winston said as he poured it into the wine glass and handed it to her. For himself he used a drinking glass which was sitting on the dresser.

"That's some good," Rita said, after drinking most of it.

"You're supposed to sip it."

He laughed and she joined in.

"I needs the Dutch courage."

"Why?"

"You knows why."

"I guess I do. I am very glad you came."

"Me, too. Thanks for being so nice to me."

"I'm having a lovely time already."

"Yeah, sure."

"It's true."

They finished eating and poured the last of the wine into their glasses. Winston opened the room door and put the tray on the carpet outside.

He stood in front of her as she sat on the bed, toying with her wine. "Are you sure?"

"Yeah. I'm sure."

"You know you can back out if you need to. I don't want to take advantage of you. You know that in a week's time I'll be back in New York and you'll be here?"

"I know. But I don't care."

He took her hand in his. It was curious, he noticed, how rough it was, presumably from years of housework, yet in a strange way it added to her attraction. He gently kissed her arm.

"Are you absolutely sure you want to do this, Rita?"

"Oh for fuck's sake, Winston. Get on with it. There's such a thing as being too much of a gentleman!"

36

Early the next morning, Katie took it into her head to thoroughly re-organize her kitchen. There was so much junk, she thought, so her first task would be to gather it up and put it on the table so it could be bagged and boxed, then taken to the tip behind Number 11. If neither the Old Bear, whose snoring she could still hear above, nor Donnie would take it to the dump, then by the jumpins she would leave it there until it rotted into the floor.

Empty jars were relatively easy items to dispense with, although some of them produced a tinge of regret since someday a use might be found for them. Bottles were different because she knew it was highly unlikely they would ever be used again. That was particularly true of a tiny, quarter–full bottle of discoloured olive oil she had bought to treat Rita's earache when she was a child, and a slightly bigger, label-less bottle with traces of a thick, black substance which she could not, and would rather not, identify.

Plates, bowls and cups were in a league of their own because, she told herself, each one—even if unusable—had sentimental value although, with few exceptions, she could not have explained why. Except the little, faded blue cup with white flowers which her mother had given her when she was a little girl. How long ago was that, she wondered? She could have been only five or six at the time.

Was that before or after the new King Edward was crowned? Or was the old Queen still on the throne? After all these years she often found it hard to distinguish between what she knew firsthand and what she had been told by her parents and others.

Katie sat on a small stool, lost in thought. She still could not believe that Queen Victoria had known and approved of all the deeds done in her name, and she was sure Her Majesty would have intervened if she had known. The strikes, the turmoil, the slack times, the closures, the marches, the deaths; and the good times, courtship, births, all drifted by in her head until she found herself weeping without really knowing why.

Suddenly she was aware that the snoring above had stopped.

She hauled herself up, feeling anew that awful pain in her left buttock and thigh, and clutched the edge of the counter for support. Dr. Green had told her it was called *piriformis syndrome*, a name given the condition by a Dr. Robinson in 1947, and that a survey of 75 physiatrists showed the majority were unsure that piriformis syndrome even existed. Why Dr. Green thought she would want to know those details was beyond her. All she knew was that the condition *was* real and she wanted a cure, which was not forthcoming.

Balancing herself on the stool, she reached to her topmost shelf to find two balls of string, a spoon Murdoch had thrown there in a fit of temper some years before, old flypapers in disgusting condition and a number of back editions of the *Cape Breton Post*, thickly coated with the dust of time.

She grabbed the nearest one and thumped it on the edge of the shelf. The dust billowed out of it and almost caused her to choke.

She saw from the front page it was dated October 31, 1956, and that the headline was *Tories Win Nova Scotia after 23 Years out of Power. Stanfield elated.*

She dropped it onto the counter, wondering why Murdoch had saved it, as it did not have good news for the CCF, the party he supported. They had been reduced from two seats to one, and lost their leader, Russell Cunningham, who had represented Glace Bay in the legislature since 1945.

She heard the door open and looked down to see Murdoch stick his head in and peer round. Seeing that Katie was alone in the kitchen he merely grunted and backed away into the living room.

"Oh, not speaking now, are we?" she shouted. "Childish as well as stubborn, hey?"

She heard the front door slam. There seemed to be a lot of slamming going on lately, she thought. Pretty soon they would have that door off its hinges.

Murdoch, who had heard her comment, made his reply where he knew she could not hear him. He waited until the door had shut behind him before unburdening himself.

"Jesus Murphy! Who the hell'd want to speak to a foolish, nagging old bag like you?"

"My God, Murdick," said Alex, who was sitting on his front steps. "Those are some harsh words to be starting off the day with."

"What the hell do you think you're doin'?" Murdoch whirled around. "Spyin' and eavesdroppin' on people now?"

He thundered away to the gate, but seeing Violet across the road, stopped and walked over to her.

"Good day, Violet."

"Good day, Murdick. I just come home to get a few things, then I'm heading back to the hospital."

"How is she? Any sign of improvement?"

"No. No she's after getting worse by the day."

"Jesus, I'm so sorry, Vi."

'The nurses will only let me in to see her for a few minutes at a time. They got all kinds of tubes coming out of her."

"Is there anything I can do?"

"No, thanks, Murdick. I gotta get back. Here's my taxi now."

Murdoch watched her go and wondered if it was true that God

took those whom he most loved because he wanted them to be with Him.

Turning in the other direction, he saw Rita coming up the row. She had changed back into her regular clothes and removed her make-up so she was not as conspicuous as she had been in Sydney the previous day, but was an unusual sight nonetheless.

"Rita! What you doin'? I didn't hear you go out."

"Morning, daddy."

"The store ain't open yet."

"No. I don't think it is."

"Then where you been?"

"Stop givin' me the third degree, will you? I stayed over in Sydney last night."

"Did you, by God. Where? Who with?"

"None of your damn business!" she snapped. "Now get out of the way, you old fart!"

Dumbfounded, Murdoch stepped aside and let her pass. Suddenly it seemed as if everyone was angry with him, and he could not fathom what he had done to deserve the world turning against him.

"'Mornin' Rita," said Alex as he walked to the fence.

"'Mornin', Alec. How's she goin'?"

"Good, b'y. You're looking some good today, Rita. You must have been up to somethin' thass done you a power of good."

"Oh," Rita blushed furiously, "just seein' some old girlfriends in Sydney."

"You should do it more often. It suits you." He dropped his voice. "Old misery guts is in a bad mood today."

"Is he ever."

"Just a word to the wise, Rita. They must have had a ding-dong, so I imagine Katie's none too happy either."

"Thanks for the warnin', Alec. But I ain't exactly sweetness and light meself. Anyone thinkin' they can use me as a doormat today better look out."

"My God, Rita, you're right impressive when your dander is up. I never seen you like this before."

"Well, there's a lot of me you never seen before."

But I wish I did, Alex thought, but did not say, as Rita let herself into the house.

37

When Rita went to the kitchen, she had to push aside boxes and pots which Katie had piled against the door. Her mother was on her hands and knees, surrounded by household items, with her head in one of the cupboards.

"Good day, Ma."

Not being able to hear, Katie continued to ferret inside the closet, banging some saucepans with her elbows as she worked.

"MA!"

Katie stopped, crawled backwards for a few feet, and then hauled herself up, sweating and panting. "Oh, it's you."

She wiped her face on her apron. "Where in the name of time have you been? I looked in your room earlier and seen your bed wasn't slept in."

"In Sydney. Like I told you, I stayed over with Rosie."

"I don't recall you tellin' me anythin' of the kind."

"Well I did."

"Did you now? How's Rosie?"

"She's good." Not wanting to extend the conversation about Rosie, Rita moved on rapidly. "What in the name of God are you doin', Ma? The place looks like Hiroshima after the atom bomb."

"I'll do what I like in me own kitchen. And I won't be after takin' orders from me own children."

Holding her hip with her hand, Katie hobbled over to the table, moved a box of Carnation dried milk powder from a chair and sat down. She took off her glasses, wiped them clean of dust and sweat, then replaced them and stared hard at Rita.

"Lord Jesus! What have you been doing to yourself? You're all tarted up like a dog's breakfast."

"I just thought it was time to get a make-over."

"Make-over? Is that what you call it? What will they think of next?" She rearranged herself in the chair, as her piriformis syndrome was striking her with a vengeance. "Ain't you goin' to work today? Or you goin' to take another day off?"

"No, I'm goin' in this afternoon."

"Is that right? Seen your father?"

"Yeah. He was out in the row when I come home."

"Good place for him!"

"You had another fight?"

"You could say that. We had a real barney last night, and this mornin' he stormed out without so much as a word."

"Dotty's letter again, huh?"

"How many times do I have to tell you, her name is Dorothy?"

"Alright, alright."

"Yeah. And after he had a go at me, he went after Donnie. Really hauled him over the coals. Hootin' and hollerin' at the top of his lungs."

"Poor Donnie. What did he do—get in the line of fire?"

"Oh, your father was rantin' about some conspiracy. He got all riled up about Donnie getting the..." Katie froze, immediately aware that she was entering dangerous territory because she had overlooked an important reality.

"About getting what?"

Kate said nothing and bent over to stroke her rheumatic leg.

"About what, Ma?"

"Best let it alone. I wants a bit of peace. Besides, look at all this work I gotta do."

"Tell me, Ma." Now aroused, Rita was in no mood to let the matter rest. She leaned over the sauce bottles and jam jars on the table and looked her mother full in the face. "Givin' Donnie what?"

"Don't be badgering me, girl." Katie started to weep.

"What?"

"Oh, well, it's just that if your father and me went to live with Dorothy and Tom...if he's ever goin' to get married...I thought as... well, him and Annie are goin' to need somewhere to live."

"So!" Rita, stood up, her anger rising. "That was the plan, was it? He's goin' to get the house. How friggin' cozy!"

"Oh, now look, Rita, please..." Katie was almost pleading for forgiveness. She could not think how she and Dorothy had forgotten the other factor in the equation.

"What about me, Ma? Did you ever give a thought to me?"

"Oh, Rita..."

"What about me, for God's sake? Was you goin' to throw me out on the street? Is that all I'm good for?"

"There's no reason you'd have to go anywhere," said Katie, hastily temporizing. "You could carry on livin' here."

"As a fucking lodger?"

"Oh, Rita, don't."

"As Annie's lodger! Ma, you knows I can't stand that woman. How long do you think it would be before she got Donnie to put me out?"

"I'm sure you're exaggeratin', Rita."

"Exaggeratin'?" Rita was now beside herself, angrily pacing the floor, knocking pots and pans left and right. "And tell me this, you old witch, why should *he* get the house? Why not *me*? I'm older than him and by rights it should come to me if it's goin' anywhere!"

Katie looked plaintively at her aggrieved daughter and burst into tears again.

"Why's he so special, huh? 'Cause he's the *baby*? Yeah, that's what it is! It was always the same…always the same."

"Now hold on, Rita—"

"Yez didn't even think of me, did yez? None of yez. Didn't even give Rita a passin' thought."

"Oh, Rita—"

"Frig yez! Frig the fuckin' lot of yez!"

Rita strode through the kitchen, kicking over any items still standing, through the living room, and out the front door.

Katie heard her leave, and sniffed, "The way things is goin', that old door ain't goin' to be long for this world. It's pr'a'lly hanging on by the one hinge."

As Rita stormed out of the house, Alex was walking down the row, carrying a bag of groceries. Rita was so full of rage she did not see him and crashed into him, knocking the shopping onto the street.

"Whoa! Where's the fire at, girl?"

"Look where you're goin', can't you?" she snapped.

"My God, Rita," Alex said, noticing her altered appearance, "you look some lovely. You looks like a movie star."

"You can keep our friggin' sarcastic comments to yourself!"

"I'm sorry, Rita. I didn't mean nothin' by it. You do look great. I means it."

Hurt, Alex stopped and started to pick up his scattered groceries.

Rita hesitated, then dropped to her knee to help him. "No, it was my fault, Alec. I was on the rampage. I just had a barney with the old woman."

"Quite a few barneys goin' on in your place recently."

"Yeah. It's all about our Dotty askin' the old folk to go live with them."

"Ah, I heard all about that from Murdick. Any new developments?"

"Just that they all got it figured out for Donnie to get the house and put me on the friggin' street."

"No!"

"Thass the way it looks, b'y."

"Rita, if I had my way you'd never be without a home, so long as I got one."

If you moved in with me this very minute, I would be over the moon, he thought, but did not say.

"Why, Alec. What a nice thing to say. You're so kind, b'y."

Yes, she thought, but did not say, he is very kind. He would make someone a far better husband than hundreds of others she could think of.

"Well, if worst comes to worst, I'll come and bunk up with Evangeline. I'd best be movin' or I'll be late for work. I'll see you, Alec."

"Yeah, see you, Rita." he said softly, sadly.

38

Before Winston left the Isle Royale Hotel he had to make a long distance call to Dan Petrie in California. He needed to clarify his mission, as Dan had left it somewhat ambiguous when they had last spoken.

While the operator was arranging his call, he gazed out of the window and savoured last night's experience. The night with Rita had been extraordinary for a number of reasons, not least for the outburst of passion from a woman who had seemed shy, withdrawn and insecure. Winston marvelled that Rita had so little experience with men, had never been married or formed an attachment of any kind.

He realized that, sex apart, he had become inordinately fond of Rita. He had been surprised to discover that she was a woman of great spirit and intelligence, which was belied by her rough way of speaking in the local dialect. He believed she deserved to find someone who would cherish her and love her with care and kindness.

For a split second, he even entertained the notion that he might be that man. But, no, he knew that could not work. They came from two entirely different spheres. So different that, even should they form a liaison, it would soon fall apart.

The operator interrupted his reverie by ringing to tell him she had Mr. Petrie on the line.

"Hello, Dan."

"Winston, I hear you're living the life of Riley up there in my hometown."

"Not exactly. How are things in LA?"

"Going through a bit of a dry period since *The Spy with the Cold Nose*."

"Yeah. I heard that it didn't get a particularly good reception."

"Hell, no. One critic said: 'Rather painful, overacted and overwritten farce full of obvious jokes masquerading as satire.'"

"Ouch!"

"Win some, lose some."

"I called because we left my terms of reference kind of loose when we last spoke."

"I was thinking about that. You've been there a few days now. What do you think? Are there any stories to be told?"

"I would say there are dozens. But are they the right kind?"

"That's the thing that's been bothering me. As you know, before I can even think about a production, I've got to know if I can find the money."

"How much are we looking at?"

"It depends on who I can get to star in it, but I figure I might be able to do it for around \$3 million."[1]

"But apart from the star or stars, you will need to pitch it to potential investors."

"Right, and they will want more than Cape Breton scenery and honest faces."

"In other words, action?"

"Right."

"I see. What did you have in mind?'

"When I was doing my Master's at Columbia, there was some kind of murder in The Bay when two Jewish people were killed by

---

1   *The Bay Boy*, the film which was eventually made in 1983 cost \$4,248,00 CA, but had box office receipts of only \$163,000.

a cop. Could you dig around and let me know what you find?"

"Sure. What year was that?"

"I would have been about twenty, so I should think it was something like 1940."

"Okay. To be clear: You just want me to get the material. You don't want me to write a script?"

"No, I'm going to do that. I want you to get the facts and prepare a treatment I can use when I come to pitch it."

"Got it. Take care, Dan. Give my love to Dorothea."

Winston had intended to spend another day with Alex, but in light of his phone conversation with Dan, he decided to call and postpone it.

So, instead of going directly to Glace Bay he walked a few yards along Dorchester Street to the *Cape Breton Post* offices and asked if he could look at back issues in order to do his research. The receptionist said she was unsure and that he had better see the editor. She called up to his office and then told Winston to go up.

"Good morning, I'm Ian MacNeil," said the editor, a friendly but slightly-harried looking man in his shirt sleeves. "What can I do for you?"

Winston told MacNeil what Dan had related to him and indicated that it was possible a movie could result from his research. MacNeil was on his feet and immediately stalked the length of the office to a huge chest of very wide drawers.

"I know what you're referring to. Of course it was before my time, but it would have been around the time Mr. Duchemin became the publisher."

"Mr. Duchemin?"

"He's the current owner and publisher. Let me see now."

MacNeil opened and closed several drawers in succession, until finally he stopped and withdrew an armful of opened newspapers.

"That was in 1940 or 1941, I think. That would have made the front page, not the Glace Bay page...yes, here we are June 18, 1941....No, I was wrong...not on the front page...yes, on the Glace Bay page. *Witnesses Accuse Policeman in Glace Bay Crime. Five witnesses say they saw him leave the scene after double murder*...and then, on June 30 of that year, *Sergeant Arthur Frost of the Glace Bay town police was committed for Supreme Court trial today on charges of murdering Mr. and Mrs Hyman Brody.* If you want, drag up that stool and you can make notes."

"Thank you, Mr. MacNeil. You've been very helpful."

"I'll leave you to it. I've got to go and see to a problem with the print setters."

Winston filled several pages of his notebook with information, including the names of the witnesses who appeared in court against Frost. They were Alex Thomas, John McNeil, Wilmena Budge and Marguerite MacDonald. Were any of these people still alive, he wondered, and if so could they be found?

Looking further on through the *Post*'s pages, he saw that Frost had been acquitted on the grounds of insanity and had been re-manded to an asylum, and that there had been speculation he had not been found guilty because of anti-Semitism which was preval-ent at the time.

Winston returned to his hotel room and called Alex to say that he would be out very soon after all. Then he looked through the Glace Bay pages of the Maritime Tel and Tel directory to see if any of the witness's telephone numbers were available.

There were no entries for Alex Thomas, several for John McNeil —which was an extremely common name in Cape Breton—one M. MacDonald, who might be anyone, and a W. Budge, which might, or might not, be promising.

Armed with the results of his preliminary research, he headed for his car.

As he started the engine, he remembered that he had undertaken to Annie to go to the Savoy Theatre tonight to hear John Allen Cameron. He had no idea what that would be all about and was not much looking forward to it, but reminded himself that a promise was a promise, and that keeping a promise could have its rewards..

39

Winston met Alex at "Stalag 13" in New Aberdeen and, while they drove into town, told him of the new assignment, asking if Alex would be able to assist.

"Jesus, b'y, thass thirty years ago. I was only in me early teens at the time. I remember somethin' 'bout it, but I can't think on what it was right now."

"Did you know or meet someone who was at the trial?"

"In Sydney?"

"I think that's where it was held, yes."

"Dunno. Don't think so."

"Was it something to do with one of the witnesses? One of the people who testified they saw the murder."

"Thass it! Yes, I remembers me old man saying that a feller was boastin' 'bout having seen it happen."

"Where was this?"

"Dunno. In the tavern, I guess."

"Can you recall his name?"

"I think it was a Thomas feller."

"Yes, Alex Thomas. He was one of the witnesses. Do you think we could find him?"

"Not around here, you won't."

"Where did he move to? Far from here?"

"Yes, b'y, he's dead." Alex cackled with laughter. "Who were the other witnesses?"

"John McNeil—"

"Only about five hundred of them in Glace Bay."

"Yes, I know. Marguerite MacDonald—"

"Same thing. Must be dozens of them."

"And the last was Wilmena Budge."

"Ah. How did they spell that?"

"B-u-d—"

"No, the other name."

"Oh. W-i-l-m-e-n-a."

"Thass wrong. The reporter pro'ly got it wrong. It likely woulda been Wilhelmina. We got a street with that name."

"So, do you know a Wilhelmina Budge?"

"Sure. Willie Budge lives in the shacks."

"The shacks?"

"It's what we calls Railway Street."

"Is she still there?"

"As far as I know. I never knew she was involved in that murder. She must be in her nineties now. I dunno if she's still all there in the head."

"Alright. Tell me where to go."

"Turn her round and go back to Number Two. When you gets to Fifth Street, turn left."

Winston made a "U" turn and followed Alex's directions. Shortly, they found themselves in an almost rural area overlooking a small lake. Some of the houses were in a bad state of repair, which no doubt accounted for the street's nickname, but none worse than the one to which Alex directed them.

Mrs. Budge was a very ancient lady, but with an active mind full of memories. She seemed pleased to be asked to tell her story, which she did with great relish.

According to her, the victims were Chaim and Chibalaya Brodie, who had come to Glace Bay—she did not know from where, she thought it might have been Russia or Poland—in the 1890s, at first raising a few cows and later opening a dry goods store and buying a small house, which they rented to Arthur Frost, who was a sergeant on the local police force.

"It all had to do with the rent," said Mrs. Budge, balancing a cup of tea on her knee, "and Art had not paid his rent for a whole year —I don't know how much it was. Imagine that! A whole year! I guess he figured that because the owners were Jewish he could get away with it."

"I don't understand," Winston said. "Why was that?"

"Oh, in them days, the Jews wasn't too pop'lar, them ownin' stores and stuff and the miners bein' poor like."

In June of 1941, Mrs Budge said that Frost "lost his rag" and was at his wit's end because he did not have the money to settle his bill. He got his gun, a hand weapon of some kind, and in a towering rage marched over to the Brodys' house.

"Me and the others seen it plain as day. 'Course, we knew he was up to no good so we followed him in and then, not minding us a bit, he shot the pair of them in cold blood."

"Good heavens," said Winston. "Did he know what he was doing? Was he drunk, do you think?"

"No he di'n't seem to be liquored up, but he di'n't care that we seen him do it."

"How old were Mr and Mrs Brody?"

"I read it in the *Post Record* at the time but I don't remember now. I think she was in her sixties and old Chaim woulda been about ten years older."

"What happened then?"

"Art turned around and marched down to the police station and surrendered hisself. Thass what they said. We di'n't follow him down there 'cause he still had the gun! We di'n't want him to be shootin' us!"

"I heard he was found not guilty by reason of insanity."

"Yes, thass right."

"Do you think he was insane, Mrs. Budge?"

"Well, he must have been, mustn't he? No sane man would do what he done."

"There was some speculation that he got off because the Brodys' were Jews."

"I can't see that. That don't make no sense to me."

"Well, thank you very much, Mrs. Budge. You've been very helpful."

"I guess when this movie is made it'll be all changed. Instead of us seein' the murder they'll have Robert Redford doin' it."[2]

"I'm afraid that will be out of my hands," said Winston with a laugh, "I'm just a lowly researcher."

They returned to their car and drove back to the Hub, where Winston dropped Alex off at his house. As he drove off he strained to see if there was any sign of Rita at the next door windows, but he saw nobody.

---

2 Mrs. Budge was right that the story was substantially changed for the movie, but it was Keifer Sutherland, not Robert Redford, who played the sole witness to the crime.

40

The Savoy Theatre was alive with light and anticipations of merriment as patrons jostled to get into line for John Allan Cameron's concert. For one night, at least, Union Street had shed its usual grey cast of mundanity and was the centre of razzle-dazzle attention. Slowly the line moved forward, until only a few stragglers were left.

Annie anxiously waited on the sidewalk a short distance away, outside the pool of light. Nervously she glanced once more at her watch, and was just about to give up waiting when Winston appeared.

"Sorry I'm late, Annie. I took the wrong turn and went up Marconi Street."

"I thought I'd been stood up," she snapped impatiently, "Come on. The curtain is about to go up!"

She hustled him into the foyer, which bore posters for forthcoming attractions. Winston noticed *Beneath the Planet of the Apes, Airport, Beyond the Valley of the Dolls* and *Patton,* several of which he had seen in New York earlier in the year.

He could see through the curtained opening that a master of ceremonies was giving an introductory speech, telling the audience that they were "in for a treat" and that, before hearing from John Allen, they would have a "grand performance" from *Moon,* a recently-formed band which included Sam Moon and Matt Minglewood, of neither of whom had Winston ever heard.

Annie dug him in the ribs and held up his ticket. "Here. This is yours. Go through now, for God's sake."

Winston did as he was told and handed his ticket to a young usher, who tore it in two and gave him back half.

As soon as they were in the auditorium, Annie pointed to her right. "Your seat is down there. Mine is across the way. I'll see you outside after."

"What about at intermission?"

"After. At the end. Outside."

Although not all to his musical tastes, Winston found the concert quite good, but he was more entertained by the audience—who were toe-tapping, hand-clapping, bouncing in their seats, and singing along—than by the performers.

On one side of him was a middle-aged man in a tartan shirt who hummed to himself through most of the songs, audibly out of tune. On the other was a buxom young woman—possibly sixteen or seventeen—on whose face was plastered a seemingly immovable grin. Two seats over to his right was another teenager, who noisily sucked her thumb throughout.

On several occasions, Winston craned his neck to look at Annie, but not once did she look in his direction.

When the lights came up at intermission, Annie was neither in her seat nor anywhere to be seen, so he aimlessly wandered about, looking at wall photos of Paul Newman, Olivia Newton-John, Jane Fonda and Dustin Hoffman.

When the intermission bell rang again, he headed back to his seat and noticed that, although Annie was in hers, she was looking directly ahead.

To rapturous applause, John Allen sang *Lord of the Dance*, and suddenly the concert was over.

When Winston stood up he could see that Annie had already vacated her seat, so he drifted to the lobby and waited there. After a few minutes, he went out into the street where it was now dark, the street lamps having just come on. Not seeing Annie among the groups of patrons who were discussing the show, he shrugged and walked away around Senator's Corner towards his parked car on York Street.

The Melody Café was in total darkness and, as Winston passed the doorway, a hand reached out and pulled him into the recess, where he found himself closely pressed against Annie's warm body.

"There you are. I thought you were goin' to be all night."

"Annie! Where'd you get to? I figured you had forgotten about me."

"No, b'y. I said I'd see you outside. This is outside."

Winston gave her a quizzical look, indicating that he wondered about the cloak and dagger theatrics.

"Gossip, Winston. We don't want to be causing all kinds of gossip. D'you understand?"

The expression on his face told her that did, and that he should have caught on long before this.

She put her key in the lock, turned it and pushed the door open. "Come on in."

Annie closed and bolted the door behind them, then led Winston through the darkened restaurant to a door at the rear. The light from the street created eerie, unreal effects as it shone through the plate glass window and cast long, weird shadows on the two furtive figures. The lower part of a painted sign on the door appeared in distorted shadow on the shiny, linoleum floor:

Everyone's happy here.
Some when they enter, some when they leave.

Annie opened the back door and pushed Winston into the blackness beyond. When she switched on the single bulb light, Winston could see that they were in a small room which served as Annie's private office and changing area. A small desk was covered with bills and other documents. There was a wooden coat stand and a waste basket in the corner, and an old couch along one wall.

She pushed him down onto the couch, straddled his knees and started to disrobe him, piece by piece.

Winston, nagged by a slight suspicion, but only a slight one, looked up at her. "You're not married are you, Annie?"

"Married? No, 'course not. What gave you that idea?"

She suddenly remembered that she still wore her engagement ring, so during a show of taking her blouse off, she reached around behind her back, slipped the ring from her finger, let it fall to the floor and kicked it under the couch.

"I just wondered. I figured a fine woman like you had to be married."

"Well, you were wrong. I have a question for you."

"What?"

"How long are you goin' to be around here?"

"I have to be honest with you, Annie. Two days, maybe three at the most."

"Well, that's alright, then."

She started kissing his chest while squirming against his lower body and limbs.

It was strange that, at odd moments like this, Winston was able to submit to the throes of passion while at the same time allowing his mind to roam to other things. It was not that he did not enjoy these encounters, but he did wonder what actual value they had. He made no claim to being a particularly moral man, and certainly was not religious (he had not attended shul for years), but he often pondered whether it was fundamentally wrong to be promiscuous.

There were exceptions, of course, when some of these amorous occasions were special, each for their own reason. Rita, he thought, had been special, but he was not exactly sure why.

Annie pulled down his pants and hurled them in the corner, while mounting him. "I see you've been done."

"Yes, I'm a Jew."

"Huh!

"We have it done when we're little. It's called a bris."

"It don't make no difference to me."

"I'm glad to know you're not prejudiced."

"Shuddup, now."

A little later, when they started again, Annie thought of something which she thought she should get settled.

"I hope you're not planning to put me in the movie," she said as she panted and rode.

"Not a chance," Winston replied. "You're secret's safe with me."

Quite soon, he would have cause to ruefully recall this hastily-made promise.

41

Donnie MacNeil, beer can in hand, had fallen asleep in front of the television, and was quietly snoring when a key in the front door lock awakened him. He shifted position and rubbed his eyes as Rita came in from her shift at the hospital.

"Oh, it's you."

"Who'd you think it was, Carol Burnett? They in bed?"

"Yeah. The old man went up hours ago, cranky as a bear. Ma went up a little while before you come in."

"Uh-huh. What are you doin'? Plottin' how to screw me seven ways to Sunday?"

"Rita!"

"Shut your mouth!"

"Look, Rita, Ma told me you was upset, but it wasn't outa spite against you. I just di'n't think of it at the time."

"Yeah, that's right. You didn't think of it!."

Rota slung her raincoat over a chair and marched up to where he was sprawled. She kicked his feet. "Good old Rita, She can go out to work to bring in money to pay the bills so you can keep more of your paycheck in your pocket. She can do housework while you sit around on your backside, swillin' beer! But when somethin' important comes along—affectin' all of us—she don't even get a thought let alone a say."

"But, Rita—"

"Thanks a million, you slimy, selfish, little bastard!"

"Oh come on now—"

"Listen to me, you little pimp." Hands on hips, she leaned over until her face was close to his. "I always looked out for you. I always took your part when the others were pickin' on you. When you had no other kids to play with, I took you to town and bought you ice cream. When you were sick, I always came and sat with you...for hours on end sometimes—"

"I know, Rita. Look, I'm sorry."

"Sorry? Sorry? So you should be, you little Jeezer. I've given up expectin' anythin' from them upstairs. Never did. As far as they're concerned, I'm just Rita the skivvy, the old maid, who should think herself lucky she got a roof over her head and be an extra pair of hands around the house."

Donnie scrunched his way to the end of the couch to avoid her hot breath.

Rita backed away from him and went to the table where she absently picked up a copy of the *Cape Breton Post* which was lying there. "See, I knows how they think. Thass how they was brought up in them days. If you was a girl you had a get married fast or go off to a convent and become a nun."

She idly rolled up the newspaper as she stalked around the room. "Otherwise you was just an old maid. An embarrassment. A fifth fucking wheel!"

"Wait now, Rita—"

"But you!" She advanced and hovered over him again. Guiltily, Donnie looked away. "But you, you little worm. I expected more from you. I was *entitled* to somethin' different from my kid brother!'

She pulled back her arm and whacked him about the head with the newspaper.

"But what did I get? Huh?"

She smacked him again, this time harder. Donnie cried out and cowered down, putting up his hands to protect himself.

"Answer me, you little weasel!"

She continued to pound him with the paper.

"Aw, lay off, Rita, for God's sake—"

Relentless, Rita rained blow upon blow until Donnie was howling with pain. From overhead came sounds indicating that they now had an audience.

"What in the name of Jesus is goin' on down there?" Murdoch's voice came through the ceiling. "For the love of God, stop that confounded racket!"

"Aw, go pound sand, you old bugger!" Rita called up, then continued to hit Donnie with the newspaper, by now in strips and tatters. "A stab in the back is all I got from you, you little rat. A stab in the fuckin' back!"

Donnie got up and ran to the door. "You're ravin' mad, Rita, that's what. I'm goin' to bed."

"So you're a coward as well as a sneak, huh?"

"Look, Rita, one way or the other, it's high time you got out on your own, anyways. If you can't find yourself a man, at least you could have some kind of a life."

"Oh. You think so, do you?"

"Yeah, I do. And you knows I'm right. You knows it yourself, Rita."

Donnie ducked out of the room and Rita hurled the ragged remains of the newspaper after him. The missile thudded against the closing door as Rita dropped to the couch and started to sob uncontrollably.

After a while, she stopped and blew her nose. Her eyes were red and her cheeks were stained with tears. She looked up and spoke into the silence of the desperately lonely room.

"Yeah, I knows it. I knows it."

42

The MacNeils' kitchen the next morning had many of the characteristics of a highly-choreographed dance, or an office of air traffic control. Murdoch, Katie and Rita were all present, but the two elders were avoiding all contact with each other, including direct conversation. This meant that Rita had to act as an interlocutor, a role she neither relished nor performed well.

She and her father sat at the table, eating toast and jam—apparently the only breakfast which was forthcoming—while Katie fussed around the stove and sink, muttering to herself.

At length, she cleared her throat and turned to face them. "Ask your father does he want more tea."

"Ask him yourself," Rita answered.

"I can get me own," growled Murdoch, hauling himself up and heading for the stove.

Katie made an elaborate gesture of getting out of his way. Murdoch grunted, poured himself a cup from the teapot and returned to the table. Katie scuttled to the wall to avoid touching him.

Shaking his head, he emitted a long rumble. "What was all that ruckus about down here last night, Rita?"

"None of our business, I figure," said Katie.

"Tell her I wasn't talkin' to her. I was talkin' to you."

"She's right," snapped Rita. "It's not your business."

"Who's *she*? The cat's mother?" Katie snarled.

"Lord Jesus, the pair of yez is like two little kids."

Murdoch glowered at his daughter as she got up to take her plate and cup to the sink. Katie made another big production about getting out of Rita's way. By way of reply, Rita threw her crockery into the sink with a clatter.

"Who's bein' a little kid now?" Katie snorted.

A knock on the front door brought them to a state of alertness. They exchanged glances, the first of the day in which they saw each other's eyes.

"Who in the hell is that?" Murdoch growled.

"I'll go," said Rita haughtily, "I'm the servant around here."

As Rita left the kitchen, Katie and Murdoch glared at each other.

"Lord, I don't know what I done to deserve this," said Katie as she wiped her hands on her apron. "A stubborn old fool and a cranky, old maid!"

Murdoch' eyes popped and he was just about to explode when Rita walked in accompanied by Violet, who was white and drawn, and wet with tears.

"It's Violet," said Rita.

"Good Day, Vi," Murdoch said tentatively.

"Hello, dear," Katie said in a low voice. "What news?"

"I thought I'd better come and tell you meself." Violet sniffed. "Margie passed away late last night. We'll be waking her tomorrow."

"Oh, Vi. I'm so sorry," Katie said.

"So am I," Murdoch said. "I spent a lot of time with that little girl. She was somethin' special, alright."

"She was very fond of you, too, Murdick. All them walks you took together meant an awful lot to her."

"Where's the wake, Vi?" Katie asked.

"At home. Tomorrow after noon."

"We'll be there, Vi."

43

Alex got up early the next day. After seeing that his mother, Evangeline, was comfortable and he had performed a few chores around the house, he set off to town to have breakfast with Winston. Following that, he planned to give the American a tour of Cape Breton Island, including what the *National Geographic* described as "the Cabot Trail, a world-famous scenic highway, runs along parts of the coastal borders on both sides of the park and crosses the highlands."

When he got to the Melody Café, he saw that Winston had not yet arrived, but three men he knew occupied a window table, drinking coffee. The most conspicuous of this trio was a renowned, outspoken battler, Jake Campbell, who owned a sprawling junkyard on the Sydney highway. He was a larger-than-life, overweight individual, whom some called a great champion of the people, and others a loudmouth know-nothing.

Campbell's more subdued and serious companions were Frazer Steele, a friendly, likeable man in his sixties with a lined, rubbery faced and curly hair; and John L. MacKinnon, a somewhat older man who was well known for his wisdom and staunch support for the CCF and NDP. Steele constantly chomped on his pipe which he periodically recharged with Edgeworth tobacco. MacKinnon spoke in a clear, ordered voice and gave emphasis to his words with a mobile index finger.

"Alec!" called Jake. "C'mon and siddown. Have a coffee b'y."

"I'm supposed to meet a feller here, but I'll sit with yez a while." Alex replied. "What are yez talking about? You settin' the world to rights?"

"First," said Campbell, "I was tellin' these two about how there's more kids around my place than you can shake a stick at. I dunno where they all comes from. Puttin' a bun of bread on the table at my house is like droppin' the puck at Madison Square Garden."

Alex joined in the general laughter as he pulled up a chair and sat down.

"So nothin' serious then?"

"Yeah there's serious matters. We got two items under discussion," Campbell said. "The first is televisions in the hospitals and the second is how Bull Marsh is leadin' the miners astray."

"Holy cow! So nothin' controversial."

"I'm saying, b'ys,"Campbell went on, "that every patient in the hospital should have a TV, but the lice that's in charge makes them pay to get it."

"I'd have thought the hospital couldn't afford to get a TV for everyone. I think yez are bein' a bit harsh there, Jakie." Alex offered.

"And don't forget," said Steele, "there's lots of patients who don't want to be bothered by a TV. They wants to rest."

"No b'y." Campbell roared, "They're lice, just lice!"

"We'll have to agree to disagree," Said Johnny MacKinnon, always level-headed and polite.

"And we'll have to agree to disagree on Bull Marsh, too," said Frazer Steele, taking up the cause of the man who had been president of District 26 of the United Mineworkers for the previous twelve years. "He's doing his best under difficult circumstances."

"On balance, I would have to agree with that," said MacKinnon.

"No b'ys, Marsh is just lice. Lice!"

Steele, who was facing the window, saw a middle aged, bouncy, stocky man, with a scar on his face, crossing the street and heading directly for the café.

"You can tell him to his face, if yez want. Thass him comin' now."

With difficulty, Campbell swivelled around in his chair to see if Steele was right. Sure enough, the stocky man was opening the door.

It was William H. Marsh, the object of Campbell's invective. Marsh was a man who had what some call 'presence'. If he was in a room, one knew it instinctively. He immediately commanded attention and when he spoke people listened. He had a deep, soothing voice when he wanted to be pleasant, but a harsh, booming one when roused—or when pretending to be roused. Marsh was a great politician, much more astute than most actual politicians, who had come from humble beginnings and had worked in Number 16 colliery in New Waterford before defeating "Honest Tom" MacLachlan for the union leadership in 1958.

Marsh used to say that if he saw a miner on the other side of the street he would always call out and wave, but if the miner was with his wife, he would cross over and praise the miner to her. It was a matter of opinion how effective "Bull" had been as union boss, but at a time when the coal industry was in decline it would have been difficult for any union president to pry huge increases in pay from management.

"My ears were burning!" Marsh said as he stood in the doorway. "I know you were talking about me."

"Morning Bull," said MacKinnon.

"'Lo Bill," said Steele.

"Boys," Marsh nodded.

"Good morning, Mr. Marsh." said Annie. "Can I get you a cup of coffee?"

"'Morning Annie. Nothing for me, thank you," said Marsh as he moved towards the men at the table.

"I was talking about yez alright," said Campbell. "I b'lieve the men could do a lot better'n you to lead them."

"I thought my ears could hear your slander from across the street, Jake Campbell." His voice became a roar as he took up a stance, rather like a boxer. "Now you listen to me, you cur. I got the only job which you don't need education for. I fought for it! I got it! And I'm *keepin'* it!"

Marsh turned on heel and marched out, colliding with Winston who was in the doorway. Bewildered, Winston watched Marsh cross the street to his office, then entered.

"Good morning everyone. What's going on?"

The three women simultaneously returned his greeting and rushed forward to wait on him. Fiercely, Annie stopped Gloria and Marlene, and directed them to other duties.

"Have this table, Winston."

"Thanks Annie. Alec, are you joining me or chewing the fat with your buddies."

"I'm comin'. I could use a good breakfast right about now." He walked over and sat down. "You missed a bit of a show just now."

"So I gathered. What was it about?"

"Oh, union politics. Jakie—thasss the big feller over there—was havin' a go at Bull Marsh, the union president."

"Ah. Is he going to run against him?"

"What, Jakie run against Bull? I never thought of it. But now you come to mention it, I shouldn't be surprised if he did one of those days."

"What are you havin' boys?" Annie inquired.

"The works, I guess," said Winston.

"Me too, Annie. Eggs over easy please."

"I don't have to ask you Winston," Annie said in a tone which Alex found strange "I know you like things over easy."

"So, what's the plan for today, Alec?"

"I thought we'd go around the Island. You got to see the Bras

D'Or lakes and the Trail. Would that be alright?"

"If you say so. It sounds fine to me. Can we do it all in one day?"

"Just about. Likely we'll get in late. If that's okay."

"Sure. Let's do it."

When they had finished eating, they said goodbye to Jake, Frazer and Johnny, and Winston rummaged in his pockets for money to pay the bill. He counted out several notes and added change, laying it out on the counter. Before scooping the money up and placing it in the till, Gloria leaned across to Winston.

"See you Winston. Don't be doin' nothin' I wouldn't do," she said with a pronounced wink. Before an uneasy Winston could answer she added, "That gives you a lot of leeway, don't it?"

Winston frowned, grunted and made for the door. When they were out on the street and were walking towards the car, Alex turned to him.

"I couldn't help noticing that Gloria back there."

"Oh yeah?

"Somethin' goin' on there I don't know about, b'y?"

"Can't say. I'm sworn to secrecy."

"Ahah. Say no more. Well, well, well, you old dog."

"We better get going if we want to be back before midnight," said Winston, unlocking and getting into the car.

44

Alex's plan was to go to Ingonish, on the northeast coast of Cape Breton, where they could have lunch, and then cross over the top of the island and return via the west coast.

As they drove out of town, Winston noticed that some houses had large signs erected on their lawns. They said:

Akerman for Action

"What are these signs about, Alec?"

"It looks like there's an election coming up. Seems like this feller is trying to get the jump."

"Who is he?"

"Some young feller used to be on the radio here. You know, one of them talk shows. But he's from away. From Wales, they say."

"Does he have a chance? Being from away?"

"Maybe, but Layton—thass the sittin' member—he's well-liked. Used to be a great ball player."

"This Layton: he's on the government side?"

"Yes. He was Minister of Labour. Maybe he still is."

"You're not sure?"

"Well, like I say, he's well-liked, but you don't hear nothing about him. He don't say much in the legislature."

"How long's he been there?"

"'Bout fifteen years, I guess"[3]

They cleared Sydney and headed for the Seal Island Bridge, which Alex said was the beginning of the Cape Breton Highlands. As they passed through a place called Little Bras D'Or, Winston was greatly amused to see a restaurant called A & K Lick-A-Chick.

Once over the bridge, they ascended Kelly's Mountain, then dropped down to St. Ann's Bay. For the first time Winston became aware of why so many people described Cape Breton as a beautiful place. These rural areas, he mused, were certainly very different from the grimy, black mining towns with their company houses and occasional remnants of the industrial revolution.

As they waited in line for the ferry at Englishtown, Alex considered whether he should pursue the matter of Winston's love life, finally deciding that if his friend did not want to talk about it, he would say so.

"I gotta hand it to you. You're a real operator. You and Gloria Maddin, huh? Who'd have thought it?"

"Ah well..."

"When did it happen?"

"Three nights ago, I guess. But keep it to yourself, Alec."

"Your secret's safe with me, b'y. Imagine! You pullin' the young ones. Must be the fancy car that does it."

Once on the ferry, despite its being a very short journey, they got out of the car and hung over the rails to watch the water roil around the boat.

"What I told you about that, Alec. You will keep it in confidence?"

"I already said I would."

---

3 The results of the election, which was held on October13, were:

Akerman, Jeremy	5334	New Democratic Party
Fergusson, Layton	3807	Progressive Conservative
MacKay, Robert	2037	Liberal

"Good. Thanks."

"Why all the top security?"

"It's kind of complicated. If it got out it could lead to an all-out war in the café."

Alex frowned and scratched his head. He stared at Winston. "I don't get it."

"Ah, well, I may as well tell you. But you have to keep it to yourself."

"So you keep sayin'. What is it?"

"I had it off with the other one at the café the other night."

"What? *With little Marlene*??"

"No, no. The other one. Annie."

Alex's eyes widened in disbelief, and his jaw dropped.

"What's the matter now, Alec?"

"D'you know who she is, Winston?"

"What do you mean?"

"Annie. She's Donnie MacNeil's fiancée, for God's sake!"

"Oh shit!"

They climbed back into the car, drove off the ferry and on to Highway 312 North. They maintained silence for several minutes.

"I swear I had no idea," said Winston quietly. "She didn't say anything about being engaged and she sure wasn't wearing any ring."

They pulled into a look-off and got out to admire the view. The wind was tearing at their clothing and hair. A few small fishing boats were being tossed about below them.

"Fantastic!" Winston said.

"I believe you," said Alex.

"What about?"

"About Annie Pyke. You weren't to know. I mean, how could you?"

"Well, exactly. I'm not a mind reader."

They stopped several more times so Winston could appreciate

the many spectacular vistas, and got into Ingonish just before twelve thirty. Although Alex advised against it because he had heard it was very expensive, Winston decided they would have lunch at the Keltic Lodge.

In a remarkably agreeable dining room with windows overlooking the ocean on both sides, they ordered a lunch of lobsters. Most of the other diners seemed to be wealthy American tourists.

The manager, who introduced himself as Herman Falls, visited their table and wished them well. The tables were waited on by very young women, arrayed in tartan, whom Alex said were probably students doing summer jobs.

"Enjoy your meal," said a pleasant red-head whose name tag read 'Theresa'. She laid the plates in front of them, and then opened a bottle of Chardonnay which Winston had chosen.

"Jesus, Winston. This is some fancy. I ain't used to eatin' like this. It's a good thing you're payin'."

"I owe you, Alec. You've been a terrific help to me."

'Aw, it's nothin'. I been gettin' a great charge out of it all."

"How did you get to know all this, anyway...you know...about the strikes and history of the various mines?"

"Mostly from readin'. You could say I've made a bit of a study of it over the years."

"Did you go to college?"

"Who, me? No, b'y. I got half me Grade Twelve."

"What?"

"Grade Six!"

They both laughed, and Winston tucked into the lobster, which he found to be deliciously tasty and tender.

"I ran away to sea when I was a young feller," Alex continued, "Sailed around the world a bit. Then I did some hard-rock mining in Northern Ontario. Then I come back here and went down the pit. Number 20. Then I took what they calls the 'pre-retirement' pension as soon as I turned fifty because I was havin' trouble with me lungs. That was only last year."

When they had cleaned their plates and ordered dessert, they drained the bottle of wine. They were relaxed and enjoying the atmosphere.

"I've been meaning to ask you something." Winston said.

"Fire away."

"Tell me about Rita."

Alex stiffened and went pale, He looked down at the tablecloth. "What?" His voice was strained and hoarse.

"Rita. You know. Murdick's daughter. Your next-door neighbour."

"What d'you mean?" Alex's voice dropped to almost a whisper. "What d'you want to know about her?"

"Anything really. She seems to be a very interesting person."

"Yeah…I guess she is …interesting."

"And certainly very attractive."

Alex looked up and gave him a searching glance.

"Yeah, she's beautiful."

"And a very sweet person, too. Very warm and genuine."

Alex stared hard at him and frowned deeply.

"Why d'you say that?" he asked, his voice now faintly hostile. "You only met her once for a coupla minutes."

Winston suddenly realized that the conversation was no longer proceeding in a way he wanted or expected. Hastily he grabbed his wine and drank it in one gulp.

"Well," Alex persisted. "Didn't you?"

Winston could think of nothing to say to propitiate the situation. He looked at Alex, who returned his gaze until, slowly, his eyes widened and he read the truth in Winston's.

"You fucking son of a bitch!"

Alex leapt up from the table and stormed out of the dining room, through the lobby and across the forecourt, disappearing from view.

Winston sat in embarrassment, silently, cursing himself, then called for his bill, which he paid from a sheaf of banknotes. Then, wearily, he rose from the table and walked out.

He found Alex standing, stock still, by a wall overlooking the sea. Below, waves were crashing against the rocks and gulls were swooping and screeching.

Winston slowly walked up to him. "Alec…"

"You bastard!" Alex turned on him ferociously. "Goddamn you, you bastard!"

"Look, I'm sorry… I didn't know—"

"You rotten piece of shit! You think you can come swannin' in here from New York, with all your money and your friggin' fancy car, pretendin' to make friends with us, then screw every woman in sight! You make me sick, b'y, fuckin' sick!"

"Please listen to me, Alec. I didn't know there was…anything… you know…between you and Rita. Just like I didn't know about Annie being engaged to Donnie."

"There's nothin'…between Rita and me," Alex said, turning away.

"Then why are you so upset?" He stared at Alex's back. When he did not reply, the truth dawned on Winston. "Oh. Fuck. Of course."

"Yeah," Alex said very quietly.

"I'm sorry. I didn't know, Alec. You said yourself before—how could I have known?"

"Maybe you should've tried to find out before getting off with every woman in the place! Who in the Jesus do you think you are? You frigging son of a bitch!"

"Alec, I—"

"And I don't doubt you promised that all of them would get parts in the movie. Yeah, that's it, I bet! You told them all they could become movie stars!"

"That's not true. I swear it. I did not promise anything to any of

218

them."

"Why in the name of God should I believe you? You're just like all the others that come from away and exploit us. You're no better'n the coal company. We always get screwed by people from away!"

Alex turned on heel and stalked away on a path which led along a promontory stretching into the sea.

Winston watched him go, then sat on the wall and waited. When an hour had passed, Winston wondered what he should do. He hoped Alex had not done anything foolish like jump down onto the rocks.

The light was subtly changing. He knew he could not return to Glace Bay alone, but he had no idea when Alex would rejoin him.

~

Several hours later, the sun was setting in a blaze of glory when Alex unhappily sauntered back from his wanderings.

"Can I give you a ride?" Winston asked, trying to sound apologetic.

"Don't look like I got much choice. I can't afford to get a room inside and I don't fancy bein' eaten alive by the bugs outside."

"Come on, pal. Get in."

45

Mike Curry was thirty-four years old, tall, trim and dignified, all qualities required for an undertaker—or, as he would have preferred to call it, a funeral director. His grandfather had started the business and it was located in a large, old building on Main Street.

Almost his exact contemporary, Vince MacGilivary, worked at his family's funeral parkour on Brodie Avenue. Founded by his uncle, who had originally been a coal miner, their business catered largely to the Protestant community while Curry's served the Catholics.

Over the years, Mike had been obliged to deal with a number of gruesome and unpleasant tasks, including repairing and embalming men mangled in underground mining accidents, but this one was particularly distressing. When the deceased was a child it was always difficult to come to terms with the fact, and inevitably it prompted questions as to why such a young soul had been taken when many older, less worthy souls had been allowed to remain.

But this case was heartbreaking not only because Margie was such an entrancing little thing, but because Mike knew her from having seen her at the hospital on a number of occasions over the past year. She always had a cheerful greeting for Mike, and asked him why he was invariably dressed in black, a question Mike had been able to dodge by declaring that he had put on his best suit just to see her.

He had finished his work, and he and his assistant stepped back, if not to admire, then to appreciate that they had done a first-rate job. Margie lay in a tiny, expensive, white coffin with elaborate gold mouldings and handles. Mike would not charge for this; it would be his gift to the family in their grief.

Margie's lifeless face was as pale as the shiny, white, silk lining on which she had been arrayed. Her dark curls had been meticulously arranged, her eyes closed in repose and her tiny hands clasped together over her chest, a rosary carefully wound around her fingers.

Mike took one last turn around the coffin, applying small, last minute touches, then straightened up and nodded approvingly. "She's ready, Jim."

"A beautiful job, Mr. Curry, just beautiful," said his assistant.

"Yes, Jim, I think we can be proud of her."

"What you've done is the next best thing to bringing her back to life."

"I wish," said Mike solemnly.

46

It was almost black when Winston's car sped along the highway back to St. Ann's Bay. The plan to circumnavigate the island had been abandoned due to their altercation and the resulting loss of time.

For many miles they drove in complete silence with Alex, arms crossed, slumped in his seat and staring straight ahead. At length, Winston decided that they could not go on in this fashion for the entire journey.

"Listen, Alec. I want you to know that there was no seduction of any kind. No inducements were offered, no promises were made. I didn't go after those women. Each of them came on to me. I expect you to believe me."

"Do you think knowin' that makes it any easier to take? I don't. It makes it a whole lot worse."

Winston nodded. Of course, he should have known.

Finally they got back to Glace Bay, and Winston turned off Reserve Street onto King Edward Street in order to head for New Aberdeen and The Hub. They crossed Main Street, but just past Currie Street and before Sterling Road, a shambling figure lurched out of the shadows.

Winston swerved to avoid him, and in the headlights they could see it was Lonnie Kelly.

"That guy seems to pop up everywhere I go."

"He's a real pain in the arse, that guy," Alex said.

"He sure is a pest. He'll be the death of me before I'm through."

Winston drew up in front of Alex's house and switched off the engine. "Are we okay?"

Alex opened the door and put one foot on the pavement. He hesitated for a minute, then turned back. "This is the end of the road, b'y. I guess you'll be going back to New York soon anyways."

"Yes, I planned on leaving tomorrow or the day after. But on balance, I think I'd better go tomorrow."

Alex nodded.

Winston continued, "I'll come and say goodbye to the MacNeils before I head out. You too, if you can stand the sight of me."

"I don't imagine it'll kill me."

"I'm very grateful to you, Alex. You've been an enormous help and a very good friend. I'm very sorry things worked out the way they did."

"Yeah. Okay, I guess I'll see you tomorrow."

Winston watched Alex go to the door and open it. On the stoop, he stopped, turned and gave a half wave. Winston returned the gesture, then drove off.

It was very dark on the Sydney Highway, and when he passed the airport turn-off, it started to rain. Winston switched on the car radio to cheer himself up. The strains of Hank Williams filled the air.

> *You'll walk the floor, the whole night through,*
> *And your cheatin' heart will tell on you.*

47

The next day Winston drove back to Glace Bay and made his way to The Hub. He went via Sterling Road and North Street, remembering how pleasant it had been on his first day, when he had stopped and looked out at the ocean.

However, today he was greeted by warning signs, and a section of the road had been roped off. It appeared as if there had been either natural erosion or subsidence caused by old mine workings collapsing, resulting in one lane of the road having vanished onto the beach some twenty feet below.

When he reached The Hub and turned into the row, he immediately saw that he would have to park on another street, because this one was packed with cars. The sidewalks were thronged with people, some going into Violet's house, some leaving. A small knot of men in suits stood by the front gate, smoking and speaking in undertones.

Violet's husband, Gordon, was dressed in black and was greeting people at the door.

Winston put his car some distance away and, in a puzzled state, walked back to the MacNeil house and knocked on the door.

Rita answered his knocking and opened the door. "Winston, what's wrong? You got a face like a slapped arse."

"I don't understand what's going on. What is all this?"

"You haven't heard?"

"About what?"

"They're waking Margie. She's passed away. You'd better come in."

"You mean, she died?"

"Yeah, It's some sad. Come in b'y."

He stepped in and followed Rita to the kitchen.

"That's awful. When did it happen?"

"Night before last. Vi told us right after you and Alec went on your trip down north. Do yez want a cuppa tea?"

"No, no thanks. I'm very sorry to hear about little Margie. She seemed like a very sweet child."

"Yeah, she was that, alright. It was just a matter of time, but it come sooner than anyone expected."

"Where are Donnie and your parents?"

"They're next door at the wake. I was just about to go meself. Maybe you wanna come with me?"

"I'm not sure. They hardly know me…and I'm a stranger here."

"No, you'll be fine. I'm sure you'd be welcome."

They sat, both staring at the carpet. Winston noticed it was worn in one place and he wondered why in that spot and not the rest of the surface. At another time he might have asked Rita, but he felt it would not be appropriate today.

"Winston…" She cleared her throat, and he looked up. "About the other night…I hope you don't think I was too…pushy."

"No, not at all. Of course I don't think that."

I mean, it's not like I make a habit of—"

"I know."

"—walking into a strange feller's hotel room and asking him to go to bed with me. I mean…whatever did you think of me?"

"I thought you were wonderful. I still do."

"Oh." Rita blushed. "Winston, you're some kind man, and I need a bit of kindness, considerin' what's been goin' on in this house lately."

"Problems?"

"Oh yeah."

"Tell me about them."

Rita sat down and poured her heart out. She spoke to Winston as she had never spoken to anybody in her life, confiding her loneliness, her feeling of worthlessness, her feeling of being exploited, and her fears for the future.

He listened for almost half an hour, unhappily but silently observing her misery. However, he also noticed that when she referred to Alex as her only friend, her tone changed and became affectionate.

Finally, she stopped talking and sobbed into a dish towel she had been holding since his entrance.

"Rita, as I think I explained before, you know you and I couldn't have a future."

"Yeah, I know that, Winston. I knew that from the beginning. I wasn't foolin' meself."

"I wish it were otherwise. But tell me more about Alec."

"How do you mean?" Rita's blush returned, and she looked away.

"I know he's kind, and you're fond of him, but I sense there's something deeper there."

"Deeper?"

"Yes, do you think you could have a future with him?"

"With Alec? Me? He wouldn't be interested. And he's older."

"Only eleven years. That's not much if people love each other."

"Love! Jesus. Alec don't love me."

"He might. He talks about you in the same way you talk about him."

"G'way, b'y."

'It's true. If he were…inclined…would you…be interested?"

"Oh, yeah." Suddenly her face relaxed and the stress seemed to drop from her. "Would I ever!"

"In that case, Rita, take the bull by the horns. He's so shy he'll never make the first move."

"No, I couldn't."

"I guarantee that if you tell him how you feel, you won't be sorry. I'm sure he'll respond."

"Oh, God. You think?"

"I'm sure."

"Jesus, me legs have turned to jelly."

"You can do it."

"Winston, I'm shakin' life a leaf, b'y."

"I think we'd better go to the—what do you call it—the 'wake'?"

"Yes. Thass right."

"My people call it the *Shiva*. If we do it properly it lasts for seven days."

"We don't wake people that long. Usually it's just the one day. Sometimes two."

They left the house and went next door. They were welcome by Gordon and two other men in dark suits.

"Sorry for your troubles, Gordon," said Rita.

"Thanks, Rita. The women are inside." To Winston, almost as if with a hidden meaning, he said, "The guys are out the back."

After they went through the front door, they had to squeeze past Murdoch, Arthur Pyke, Billy Pittman and Layton Fergusson, MLA, who were acting as a kind of Praetorian Guard in the passage. At the end of the passage, through the open kitchen door, they could see Donnie, Annie, and Marlene watching two older women cutting sandwiches and making tea. At the first doorway on their left there was a small wooden stand on which lay a visitor's book and pen.

Beyond, in the living room, various women, Violet, Katie, Evangeline, and others, sat crammed around the walls. In the corner, against the far wall, was Margie's tiny white coffin, open from the waist up, with a padded, kneeling rail in front. On either side were cascades of flowers, white lilies most prominent among them.

As he awkwardly stood there listening, Winston thought it strange that very little of the conversations were about Margie, but about mundane topics. Several of the women seemed much exercised about rats at the dump behind Number Eleven, and were berating Donald MacInnis, the local Member of Parliament.

MacInnis, a wiry, combative man, told them it had nothing to do with him and that they should tackle their Town Councillor, Johnny Dan MacDonald. At the sound of his name, an elderly, scarlet- faced man lumbered over and was at great pains to explain that they should see Gordon Smith or Walter MacPhee, one of the councillors for Ward Four, where the dump was located.

"You politicians is all the same!" One very old woman barked. "Yez're all pissin' in the same pot, b'y!"

Winston, uncomfortable in strange surroundings and in the presence of so many people he had not met, followed Rita around the wall of seated women until they came to Violet where she gave Rita a hug.

Winston muttered what Rita had told him to say. "Sorry for your troubles, Mrs."

Then, following what others were doing, Winston went to the coffin and stared at the waxy, white, lifeless face of Margie, whom he had met once and knew only briefly when he had carried her to the ambulance. He felt that, being a Jew, he could not cross himself, so he mumbled an improvised prayer.

Winston backed into the passage, where he bumped into Arthur Pyke.

"How's she goin' b'y?"

"They're out the back, Winston," said Murdoch. "If yez wants a drink of rum."

"Thanks Murdick."

In the kitchen, Annie gave him a glance packed with meaning

and warning. She slightly twitched her left shoulder to indicate where Donnie was standing.

Winston understood. "Good day, Donnie. Annie."

"They're out in the yard," said Annie.

Apparently, having no other option, Winston pushed through the back door and into a yard which felt more like a bullring than a *Shiva*. Five men were leaning against the house, and six more, including Alex, against the fences. Another man, clearly inebriated and leaning against the gate, was ineffectually attempting to play a guitar. Almost all were smoking furiously and half had half pints of rum sticking out of their shirt pockets.

When Winston tentatively appeared, they greeted him like a long-lost relative and pressed cigarettes and rum on him.

Winston puffed on a cigarette, took one small swig of dark rum, the only kind he could stomach, and started chatting with some of the men about Dan Petrie's movie. All the while he was glancing at the door, waiting, hoping Rita would appear.

Just when he had concluded that she had panicked and would not show up, the door opened and, with a quick glance towards Alex, she came over to Winston.

"You talked me into it. This is what they calls the moment of truth. Wish me luck, b'y."

"I wish you all the luck in the world, Rita."

"Thanks, b'y"

"And, Rita…"

"Yeah?"

"I'm leaving now. I'm going to take another quick look at the town, pick up my gear, and get on the road. I'll probably stay some-where in New Brunswick tonight."

"Goodbye, Winston. I'll never forget you. Thanks for everything."

~

As Winston crept through the house, Rita took a deep breath and marched over to where Alex was standing.

"There you are, Alec. I might have known you'd be up to no good, hangin' out with this lot of layabouts."

"Rita!"

"Hey, Alec," shouted a man in a very loud plaid shirt, "sounds like you two are an old married couple, the way she's talkin' to you."

"Oh...umm..."

"Not yet," said Rita so all could hear, "but maybe soon. Come with me, my boy." She grabbed him and towed him out into the row.

"Whass this all about, Rita. Whass goin' on, girl?"

"Winston told me you got feelin's for me. Is that so?"

"Ah..."

"Well, is it?"

"You know it."

"And I told Winston that I got feelin's for you. What you got to say about that?"

"Oh, my Christ! Thass wonderful!"

"All these years and you never said anything. How come?"

"I come close to tellin' you many times. Hundreds. But I figured you'd think I was a dirty old man."

"Dirty old man, huh?" Rita cackled. "So, what're going to do about it?"

"Depends on whether you'll marry me."

"'Course I will."

"Give me a kiss then, Rita. For the love of God, give me a kiss."

48

Rita, Murdoch, Katie, Donnie and Annie sat crowded around the kitchen table, each with a teacup in front of them. The big teapot, wearing its woollen cozy, sat in the middle of the table, flanked by a sugar bowl and a jug of milk.

"Alright, Rita, you got us all here, so what's it all about?" Murdoch asked with a growl.

"That's what I want to know," echoed Annie. "I got better things to do with my time than sit around here chewin' the fat."

Donnie sensed that his sister had something important to say, and gently placed a restraining hand on Annie's arm. "Let's hear her out, hon. Go ahead, Rita. Annie don't mean no harm. We're all a bit jumpy those days."

"Alright," said Annie, shaking free from Donnie's hand, "but we better get on with it, whatever it is."

"This wasn't my idea," said Rita quietly. "I wouldn't have done it this way meself, but Winston thought it'd be better."

"Winston?" Annie said nervously. "What's he got to do with this?"

"It was his idea to get yez all together."

"Jesus, Murphy and Joseph!" Murdoch exploded. "Will you get on with it, Rita, and tell us what in the name of time all this is about!"

"Alright. Stay with me, will ya? Here's how it goes. Donnie and Annie get married—at long last—and move in here—"

"What—?" Annie exclaimed.

"But—" Katie interposed.

"Hold on one friggin' minute—" Murdoch spluttered.

"Wait now! Listen to what I'm tellin' you," Rita yelled. "Will yez all shuddup until I'm done? Now then, Ma and Daddy lives part of the year with our Dotty—"

"I wish you wouldn't call her that—" said Katie.

"Shuddup, Ma!"

"Excuse me for livin'."

"And the other part of the year here with Donnie and Annie. It's what sensible people calls a compromise."

They all stiffened and stared at Rita as if she had three heads. After a few seconds, Annie looked at her fiancé and nudged him in the ribs.

"It works for us," Donnie said firmly.

"Fine with me," said Katie with alacrity.

"Dad?" Rita leaned over to her father.

He looked down at the table top. "Jesus! Why is it always down to me?"

"What d'you say, Murdick?" Katie pleaded. "Will you do this... please, Murdick...for me?"

The sound of the wall clock had never seemed so loud, so foreboding, as they sat and waited.

Murdoch got up, shambled to the sink, and looked through the window up at the row of company houses where he had spent more than seventy years of his life.

At length, he turned and emitted a long groan. "Yez've got me outnumbered, so I may as well say yes."

There was a collective sigh of relief as Katie went over and put her arms about him. She stood on tip toes and kissed his leathery old face.

"Thank you, Murdick," she said, but then looked startled. "Wait a minute. Rita, dear, what about you? What will you do?"

"I'm movin' next door."

"*What*?" Murdoch exclaimed.

"What do you mean?" Katie demanded.

"Alex has asked me to marry him."

"Jumpin' Joe Jesus!" Murdoch smiled broadly. "Well, I'll be fucked!"

Katie walked over and gave her daughter a squeeze and a kiss.

49

Dusk was gathering as Winston wound his way out of town. The sights and sounds of Margie's wake—the like of which he had never before experienced—were still with him, as were thoughts of Rita. Dear Rita. A tear ran down his cheek as he earnestly hoped her life with Alex would be long and content.

He switched on the radio. They were playing Hank Williams again. Winston had noticed that Williams and Jim Reeves were very popular in Cape Breton. He turned up the sound. It was the same song he had heard recently.

> *Your cheatin' heart will make you weep*
> *You'll cry and cry and try to sleep*
> *But sleep won't come the whole night through*
> *Your cheatin' heart will tell on you.*

A pink sun was setting fast as Winston turned off Roost Street onto North Street to face a darkening ocean. He told himself he would stop and look at the sea as he had on that first day in Glace Bay.

He was about to slow down when suddenly Lonnie Kelly lurched out of Ocean Avenue and stumbled towards the car.

To avoid the drunken man, Winston swerved violently, crashed through the barrier where the road had eroded, and dropped headlong onto the rocks below.

He was killed instantly.

AN DEIREADH

Jeremy Akerman

About the author

Jeremy Akerman is an adoptive Nova Scotian who has lived in the province since 1964. In that time he has been an archaeologist, a radio announcer, a politician, a senior civil servant, a newspaper editor and a film actor.

He is painter of landscapes and portraits, a singer of Irish folk songs, a lover of wine, and a devotee of history, especially of the British Labour Party.

Jeremy's first novel, *Black Around the Eyes,* was published in 1981. Other projects required his intention until recently, when he was able to take up fiction again. From the start of 2023 to the summer of 2025, he wrote and published eleven novels.

See: moosehousepress.com/authors/jeremy-akerman